Runcina Terrae

The Clarion Call

Book 2

By Robert Krause

RUNCINA TERRAE

The Clarion Call

Copyright © 2022

ISBN 978-1-7379888-2-3

Art by: Adrian Doan Kim (adriandkc.com)

Publisher: Piper Publishing, LLC (piperpublishing.org)

10 9 8 7 6 5 4 3 2

Runcina Terrae

For family. ILU

1 m = 3.2 feet
1 km = 0.6 miles
Western Ocean
Northern
Magnus Frater
West Fork Town
West Fork River
Occursum
Ventus
South Fork River
Oram Septentrionalis
Western Mountains
Mächtige Mauer
Meridiem
Ocram Meridionalis
Fairharbour
Southern Sea

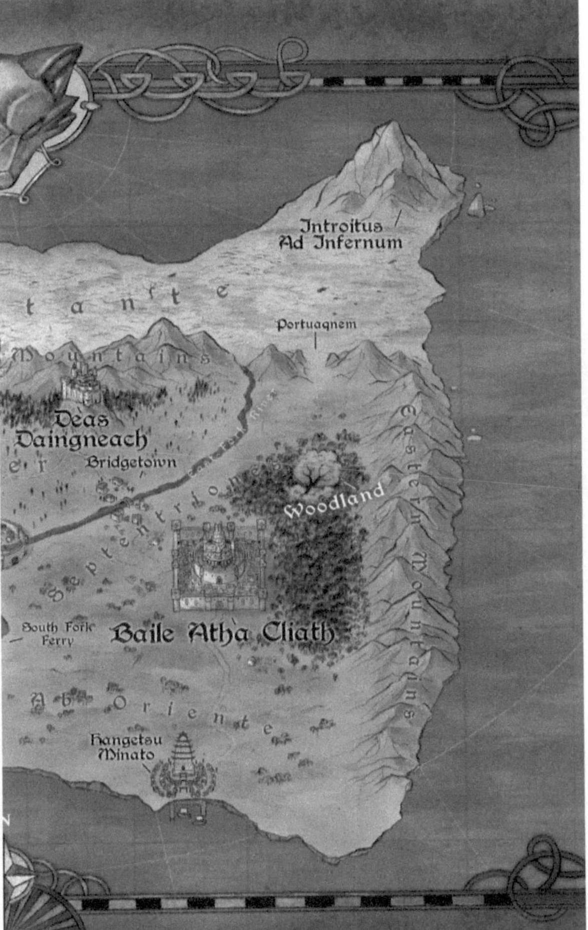

Introitus
Ad Infernum
Portuagnem
Mountains
Deas
Daingneach
Bridgetown
Woodland
Eastern Mountains
South Fork
Ferry
Baile Atha Cliath
Ab Oriente
Hangetsu
Minato

Table Of Contents

<u>Chapter 1</u>

H e waited behind his black lacquered desk; each of the four legs of the desk was innately carved with heads of animals intertwined in a dance of survival of predator and prey long since gone to time. His elbows on the desk and his hands steepled, he was lost in thought, staring blankly out into the empty room devoid of any furniture save the ornate desk and matching high backed ladder chair. There were no windows to let in any light, only four large fireplaces, one in the middle of each wall, roaring with life and devoid of warmth. The walls, floor, and ceiling were all black tile polished to a mirror shine. He could feel the presence of the minds he had seduced and trapped in the next room. He also felt the black link to his master; the power it gave him was exquisite; the joy of pain he had grown accustomed to; the price of immortality and what he now thought was sanity.

The reality was this room, and the next was all a construct of his consciousness; his true body was endlessly floating in an eternal slumber. The harsh truth of this nothingness. His prison for millennia. The void. Stuck between one plane of existence and another. *I will make Marcus Ulpius Trajanus pay,* he thought, scowling behind his red-lacquered mask. *I will make his kin and all that stand with them pay.* Then, with a most wicked idea, he smiled a devious smile.

He looked at the wall across from his desk, and with very little concentration needed, the wall shimmered and changed. The fireplace was gone, now replaced with a plain ebony door. He knew these weaves so well; it was almost instinctual and automatic. Reaching out with his thoughts, he found the poor trapped mind.

"COME!" His thought boomed in the helpless mind of his quarry.

She had no choice but to jump and obey, like a new recruit in the military or a First Year in Occursum. As she walked to the door, she checked her hood to make sure it was pulled over her head enough and adjusted her black velvet mask that hid her round apple face. She took a last deep breath; the odd combination of spicy incense and brimstone burned her nostrils and the back of her throat as she turned the brass door handle. *This could be my last,* she ominously thought.

Once she stepped through the doorway and closed the door, the wall shimmered and returned to its original state with the fireplace. A slight shiver ran down her spine. Even though this was not her first summons, knowing death here was as permanent as real death, the idea of it rattled her. The sleeping body would just cease to work, and it would look like a natural death. No one here but the man behind the desk used real names. He liked to keep it that way. That was one of many rules he had. Adherence to the rules meant favor, favor meant advancement, and advancement meant power. The lowest stable hand, poor, or beggar could have more 'power' than a King or Queen here; if the man behind the desk deemed it so, if Aires declared it so.

She quickly walked to the center of the room and prostrated herself down on hands and knees on the slick, cold floor in homage to Aires. He let her remain there for several minutes, studying her, allowing her to feel what she thought was physical discomfort on the tile floor.

"Rise, my daughter," he said. His voice slid into her mind like oily mucus from a slug. Oh, how he enjoyed making these inferior beings squirm.

The corpulent woman struggled to stand as she was in an uncomfortable position for a while, and her joints stiffened.

"What is thy bidding, my Master," she breathed from her effort of standing and reviling from his commands in her head.

"You will return to the Spire. Gather the following *sisters*: Gildred Quia, Hamala Quia, Junis Quia, and Kaylee Quia. Retrieve a Medi Obiectum that looks like a small grey granite chess pawn. You know of which I speak. Tell the four to travel light and fast to southern Ventus, just north of the Meridiem border. In a small farming village there, find a young man named Joesiph Williams. He has Medeis and potential. Once found, take him to the Meridiem border and meet up with my emissary and his host from the south. He will give commands from there on in my name."

The corpulent woman in the black velvet mask took in the command and tried not to wince as it seared into her brain; Aires ensured his orders were not forgotten to the letter.

"As you wish, my Master," she said as she gave a low sweeping bow.

Aires released her mind from the void before she could recover from the bow. *Ugh, these so-called Quia,* he disgustedly thought, *fodder for the line. Soon…yes, soon the way will open,* he thought while looking up at the ceiling, and the devilish smile reappeared behind his red-lacquered mask.

Aileen Quia awoke and bolted upright in her room. She was drenched with sweat, and her small clothes were stuck to her like a second skin. She reached out with Medeis and lit a small candle on her side table. It didn't offer much illumination but allowed her eyes to adjust enough from the pitch black to see the rough outlines of the furniture in the room. She put her head in her hands, the pain of the commands still burning like a hot knife in each temple and behind each eye. She knew with time, the pain would subside, but the message would not. This was not her first directive. She had others and deftly carried them out. Raising her to the status of command. She was immensely proud of her efficiency, would do anything to hold onto the power, would *kill* anyone that *dared* interfere with her thirst for more.

Aileen rubbed her temples and tried to work out the pain as best she could. She couldn't heal herself with Medeis, and asking one of her sisters would admit weakness. She would not lose power over a bit of pain.

Satisfied with the subsiding pain, she opened her eyes again, this time without the blinding stabbing pain in her skull. Aileen slowly swung her legs over the side of the bed and stood up, rising to all of her 5-foot height. She staggered slightly, exhausted from her ordeal in the 'dream', as she crossed the room to her wardrobe. Opening the lightly stained and well-oiled maple doors, Aileen changed her small clothes for some fresh ones. She washed her face and neck, using matching porcelain, pitcher, and basin, white with intricate brown intertwining vines along the top edges. Feeling more refreshed, she went back to the wardrobe and selected a brown dress with an A-frame neckline. After slipping on some soft slippers, she looked out her window to try and determine the time.

Still early morning, she thought as she observed no glow on the horizon from her eastern-facing window. *Not many people will be about except a few other Brown's, and maybe some Blue's doing research and experiments.*

Aileen took the small taper candle for light, softly opened her door, and looked down either way of the hall. *The fewer eyes, the better*, she thought. Her apartments were not the most elaborate, Brown Quia cared more for books than furnishings, and she preferred hers to be on the lower levels of the Spire. *Closer to my books,* she would explain whenever asked. For 200 years, she lived in the same apartment. Oh, she was offered more spacious accommodations as she rose through the ranks of her Septem. But her reasoning was always the same. *The Brown Septem should care only for books and the preservation of knowledge;* she would lecture any and all, whether they asked or not. Like many other sisters, she did her rotations in the lecture halls, but she was always more at home with her nose in a book and her garments all dusty from searching the lower basements for some forgotten tidbit.

It was one of those discovered tidbits she was now off to reacquire. A Medi Obiectum, an object of medium power. Even someone without Medeis can utilize this particularly nasty thing. She happened upon it by accident when reaching for a book on a shelf that was too high for her, resulting in a wooden box crashing down to the floor. After cursing herself for not using the step ladder, she started to pick up the nice but plain grey granite chess set. She examined each piece before putting them into a new box, thankful they were not chipped. As she placed the last piece into the box, she thought, *Bloody fool woman.* A sharp squeak came from above her head, and a large rat fell from the top shelf onto her head. After a small fright and flailing of arms about her head, she saw the rat lying on the ground. Curious, she looked closer at it. The small blood vessels in its sclera had burst, possibly indicating a heart attack. *Odd,* she thought, *why would a rat die in this manner?* She looked around to see if any other animals may have frightened the rat. There were none. Now that the adrenaline was wearing off from a rat falling on her head, she felt the pain in her hand. She opened it to see the small grey granite pawn and its imprint in her palm. *I wonder…*she mused as she tucked the pawn into a small pouch tied to her dress belt.

Aileen went out into one of the many courtyards that encircled the Spire. She walked up to one of the large maple trees, took the pawn out of her pouch and clutched it in her hand, and looked amongst the branches. Finding a small robin feeding its fledglings, she concentrated on the adult bird. *Bloody bird,* she thought. The bird, in mid-regurgitation, went wide-eyed and fell from the tree. Aileen knew then that this was possibly a relic from the War of Power. *But what to do with it?* She pondered, tucking it back into the pouch. *It could prove helpful in the future.* That was close to 100 years ago, she reminisced.

Aileen made her way silently down the stairs from her apartment to the Main Gallery and through the door leading to the storage basement floors. The lowest levels are locked and reserved as vault storage for dangerous objects and some rooms for well-guarded rites of passage. Only the Scriba Ad Primum has the keys to get down there, as well as the knowledge to get past the protection wards. But that is not where Aileen was headed.

She went down four floors and went through the door on that landing. Closing the door behind her, her small taper candlelight was in jeopardy of being swallowed up from the darkness. Aileen reached out with Medeis and lit the torches she knew very well on the long hallway walls. Like most of the Spire, the basements were carved out of the granite rock with Medeis. Smooth stone walls, floors, and ceilings. As if liquified and reformed into the Spire above. The knowledge of such use of Medeis long forgotten.

With the hallway now sufficiently illuminated, Aileen blew out her insignificant candle. The hallway floor had decades of dust on it, reassuring Aileen that her prize would be untouched. Not that she was worried, she had placed a protection ward on it. If disturbed, she would immediately know. She took a step, then paused. *Fool woman!* She scolded herself. *Acting like a bloody First year!* She cautiously reached out with Medeis to *feel* for other wards and potential traps. Satisfied in finding none, she continued down the hall. *I deserved to be caught for lighting the bloody torches without checking first!* She continued to berate herself.

Coming to a large dark oak door reinforced with iron bracing, the fifteenth door on the left, she again cautiously reached out for traps and wards. Now more confident in her approach, she gave a satisfied snort and slowly opened the door.

The room was pitch black, but the hallway torchlight illuminated the first few rows of sturdy wooden shelving. Each row of shelves was 50 feet long, 15 feet high, and consisted of many adjustable shelves of various heights depending on storage need. Aileen still used caution and reached out as she made her way to the middle of the fifth shelf on the fifth row. *Easy to remember, if the directions are easy*, she reminded herself. She found the small wooden simple pine box she had placed the pawn in and placed that in her belt pouch. She then took a book from one of the lower shelves. *Just in case some eyes were too curious,* she thought. Making her way back to the door, she again faced the room. Aileen reached out with Medeis and used a thin whisp of air to cover her tracks on the dusty floor.

Aileen did the same upon reaching the stairs' landing and snuffing out the torches by denying them oxygen and up to the second landing. From there, there were enough footprints in the dust that no one would be the wiser. She made her way back to her apartment, passing a few servants and First Years running to their morning duties and assignments. *Nobody ever looks twice at a Brown with a book,* she chuckled to herself.

Inside her apartment, she went over to her writing desk, again a plain but well-oiled piece of maple, and composed her order. Typically, the Black Septem members are unknown to each other, but Aileen had been able to discern a few members, especially over the recent years. She knew all four of the names Aires had told her; she had doled out commands to each of them separately over the years. *I had hoped for a new name,* she paused in thought as she wrote, *but I would have kept the who's who to myself as Aires did. Knowledge is power.*

Aileen finished her brief command for Gildred Quia without signing it, sanded the ink, and left her room yet again. She made her way up seven flights of sweeping wide spiral stairs that overlooked the Main Gallery to one of the floors the Red Septem used for living quarters. Septems rarely intermingled on apartment floors, but Browns seemed accepted everywhere. Mainly because they got lost frequently with a book open and their eyes down. Again, Aileen noticed that nobody paid her much attention as she found herself in front of Gildred's main door. No one locked their doors in the Spire, as it was considered one of the safest places in all the Kingdoms. She lightly knocked, listened, and went inside.

Aileen quickly closed the door behind her and found the apartment, as she expected, empty. She knew Gildred and her mate Carolee Quia would be at breakfast. *Gildred would return, and Carolee would go to the lecture hall to begin her classes for the day.* Aileen located Gildred's writing desk, a gaudy dark oak thing carved with men in various subservient poses, gilded with gold to enhance the suffering of the wooden men. Aileen shook her head at the sight, even knowing most Reds despise men for their own various reasons; very few actually choose the Red Septem to want to help men that have Medeis. She left the note and the little box on Gildred's desk, listened at the front door for any close foot falls, and quietly left the apartment.

Aileen made her way back to her apartment, satisfied her mission was successful. *Aries will be pleased*, she mused, *and I will be rewarded.* Aileen smiled at the last thought as she readied herself for some actual sleep. *A very busy and productive day and breakfast was yet to be over.*

****

Gildred and Carolee had just finished their breakfast in the main dining hall and were about to go their separate ways when Geralyn Quia came up to Gildred.

"I wonder if I could have a word, Gildred?" she asked.

"Of course, sister," Gildred replied.

Gildred turned toward Carolee, "If you will excuse us, I wouldn't want to keep you from your lecture, love."

"Of course, my heart," Carolee replied as they shared a quick kiss goodbye.

Carolee was about to turn left out of the dining hall and stopped short. *Ugh, you fool, the book is on the desk!* She quickly turned right and nearly knocked a First Year over in the process. The First Year made a squeak in startlement.

"Watch where you step, child," Carolee motherly scolded her.

"Yes, Mother. I'm sorry, Mother," the First-Year spat out as fast as she could, keeping her eyes down meekly.

Carolee continued on without caring who, what, or where the girl was and going. She had to get the book and to her lecture on time and didn't have a moment to waste on the First Year. She made it up the many flights, with many noticing she was on a mission, and gave her a wide berth.

Once inside her apartment, she went to her nice cherry wood desk, not as ornate as her love's, but what it lacked in its carving, more than made up for in its rich color, in her opinion. Carolee retrieved the book on "The Ways in Interrogation of men" and almost left the room when she noticed the small box and note on Gildred's desktop.

Curiosity getting the better of her, Carolee opened the note. Her eyes widened as she read.

"Oh, my love," came the voice behind her, "how I wish you went straight to lecture instead."

Carolee spun around and saw a cool-faced Gildred.

"What.... what is this??" Carolee sputtered in disbelief.

"It is, as it seems, love," Gildred said coolly as she made her way around Carolee to her desk.

"But...but this is impossible!" Carolee said in shock as she turned, following Gildred. "Not you! Not here!"

Gildred opened the small box on her desk and smiled. With the cool grey granite in her hand, she turned and faced Carolee.

"Ah, but yes. It *is* possible," Gildred crooned, "It *is* me, and I *am* here."

Carolee's eyes went wide. She grabbed at her left arm and chest. The note floated down onto the ground. Carolee crumpled, facedown, on the floor. Gildred tucked the pawn into her belt pouch and knelt down beside her lover's head. She brushed a few strands of hair away from Carolee's still open and wide eyes. Gildred picked up the partially crumped note from Carolee's death throws. Smiling as she read it, Gildred calmly stood up and left her apartment in search of her new companions.

Chapter 2

Gildred made her way down the seventh hall, where her apartment is, to find her first companion. This sister was the easiest to reach as they were of the same outward Septem. Hamala Quia's apartment was only a few down from her own. It was only in the last few months that Gildred had even found out that another sister from her Septem was even a Black one. Black sisters rarely, if ever, find out who each one is. It's a well-guarded secret of survival and power. *But now,* she thought, *I know five of my Black sisters.*

Gildred knocked on Hamala's door.

"Come," came a voice from inside.

Gildred opened the door and closed it behind her.

"Alone?" Gildred asked.

"Yes," Hamala said.

Gildred then did the weaves against eavesdropping.

"We can now speak candidly," Gildred announced.

"What news, sister?"

"We are to take a little trip southwest with Junis and Kaylee. Once we are outside of the Spire, I will divulge more. I will inform Junis; you will tell Kaylee. We leave at first bell tonight."

"How fast do we need to travel?"

"With most alacrity, sister. Oh, and Carolee is sadly no more."

"How unfortunate for you. My condolences."

Gildred had a small sinister half-smile form on her lips, "Thank you, sister."

Gildred left Hamala's apartment and made her way to the Main Gallery stairs. She went up to the fourteenth floor. Most sisters were about their duties by now, so the hall was empty. Gildred made her way along the long curvature of the hallway to Junis' apartment. She knew the Blue would still be gathering books and papers before going down to her laboratory. *Blues were almost as bad and absent-minded as Browns*, she thought as she shook her head slightly in disgust.

Gildred was about to knock on the door when it flung open to reveal a surprised Junis, arms full of papers and notebooks. Her high-necked blue dress was wrinkled, and there were many ink stains on the sleeves. Her short brown hair was always a rat's nest and fit right in with her usual unkempt appearance.

Junis had to crane her neck high to see Gildred's blue eyes. Gildred stared down at Junis and briefly thought of Carolee's similar green eyes. Even though they both also had brown hair, Carolee's was longer and kept in better shape. Unfortunately, that's where the similarities between the two ended. Junis was short and of a slim build. Gildred preferred women who were voluptuous, taller, and from her Red Septem.

"First bell tonight, and fast and light," Gildred quietly commanded.

"Yes, sister," Junis meekly answered.

Gildred didn't say anything else. She didn't have to. She held all the information at the moment, so that was power to her. *Let the others flounder in their suppositions*; she chuckled to herself as she made her way back along the long curved hallway to the stairs. As she descended the stairs, a First Year in white came running up to her.

"MOTHER!" she said out of breath.

"Yes, child. Out with it," Gildred annoyedly replied.

"There's been a terrible accident. You are needed in your apartment at once per the Scriba Ad Primum, Mother."

Gildred eyed the young girl like a butcher at the market. *Tall, heavy bosom, blue-eyed, perhaps she'll choose the Red*, she thought as she slightly licked her lips and felt a tingle at her waist.

"Go about your duties, child. I am on my way back now," she told the First Year.

"I am to escort you, Mother. Scriba's orders, Mother."

"Fine. Lead on, child," Gildred said, half annoyed and half happy to be able to watch the young girl walk ahead of her.

When they reached Gildred's apartment, the young girl curtsied and scurried away. Gildred took a moment to watch her silhouette as she went.

"AHEM," came a voice that burst Gildred's fantasy. She turned from the fading sight of the First Year to see the Scriba Ad Primum looking at her with those ever-judging brown eyes. At 5' 6", Genelia Quia was only a little shorter than Gildred but made up for those four inches and more in attitude. Genelia was radiant in her low-cut yellow dress with her exotic olive-brown complexion and always perfect short brown hair.

"Just because I've already eaten does not mean I can't look at the menu," Gildred chided Genelia.

"Come inside. I have disturbing news."

Gildred knew what was inside her apartment, but put on a face of worry for show. She let Genelia guide her in.

"Unfortunately, a servant found her a few hours ago when she failed to appear for her lecture. It looks as if she had a heart attack. I am very sorry, Gildred."

Gildred played the game and broke down in tears as she fell to her knees next to Carolee's sheet-covered body.

Genelia waited a couple of minutes and then reached down to grasp Gildred's shoulders. Gildred reached up with one hand and clutched tightly on Genelia's hand while covering her eyes with the other.

"Please, let me know if there is anything I can do." Genelia genuinely said with sympathy.

"Than…Thank…Thank you," Gildred said between fake sobs.

Genelia gave Gildred's shoulder a squeeze of comfort and a signal to release her clutch, which Gildred picked up on.

"I'll leave you for now, but you know where to find me," Genelia said as she turned to go.

"Yes, Scriba," Gildred replied.

Gildred waited a minute until she was sure Genelia was well gone before getting to her feet. She wiped her eyes from the few tears she could squeeze out and looked to see who else was in the room. She knew the standard procedure for death was that a Yellow and a Blue sister would come to collect the body and escort it to a room in the first basement level used for autopsies. The funeral would take place three days after the autopsy was completed. A large pyre would be held in the main courtyard of the Spire, followed by a celebration of life in the Main Gallery.

Gildred knew that she would miss the following events, which would cause great suspicion on herself, but she was done pretending. She was done with all the pretense and especially done with how things were run in the Spire. Gildred felt the world had become weak and needed to be made strong again by any means necessary. *The ends justify the means* she often told herself.

There was only one other living person in the room with Gildred at the moment, and by the look of the girl, she was a Fourth Year. *Not an especially pretty girl,* Gildred thought as she looked her up and down like she was sizing up which apple she would choose. Finally, she decided the girl was not worth another thought, knowing the Fourth Year would just silently wait for the escorts to take the body. Gildred needed to continue her dutiful role of distraught lover for only a few more hours, so she gathered herself up and made her way into the bedroom she had once shared with Carolee.

She went to Carolee's wardrobe; *ugh,* she thought, looking at it for a moment, *Such a plain hideous hunk of wood. I can't wait to never see it again.* Gildred opened the simple cherrywood doors to the wardrobe and indifferently picked out the first red dress she laid her hands on. However, she did take her time and neatly folded the dress. Typically, the body would be adorned in the deceased finest clothing and best jewelels, but Gildred was thinking about the next step. *Why waste jewelelry?* She thought *I could, and probably will need to, find its use since I won't be able to return here.*

Gildred went back into the main room with the neatly folded dress just as the escorts arrived. Dryll Quia from the Blue Septem and Erial Quia from the Yellow. *Two very efficient, respectful, and play-by-the-rules types.* Gildred fought control to not roll her eyes. She handed the dress to Erial.

"We are very sorry for your loss, Gildred," Erial said sympathetically.

Gildred made a feigned sniffle, "Thank you, Erial."

Gildred saw the glow of Medeis form around Dryll as the covered corpse of Carolee Quia was lifted in the air on gentle threads of Air. Dryll and Erial made small curtsies toward Gildred and followed the body out of the room.

The Fourth Year did the same. Gildred was now alone, finally.

She closed the door to her apartment, reached out with Medeis to light the fireplace, and threw the note into the flames. She watched it burn, not with any sadness, but the satisfaction that it burned completely. Gildred then went into her room to pack for her mission, and her flight from what she perceived was captivity. No one would come to pester her about funeral details until tomorrow, the day of her freedom, the day of her final rebirth to be who she was meant to be.

Chapter 3

The sun had finally set about three hours ago. The bell at the apex of the Spire had rung twelve times. Midnight. One hour of arduous waiting left to go. Gildred had her waterproofed leather travel bag ready an hour since they took Carolee. Two changes of clothes, and all the jewelelry she could find, just in case the gold she hoarded ever ran out. That was probably her most significant concern, balancing how much Occursum gold versus its weight was in her bag. Sometimes jewelelry was less traceable and therefore more versatile. She hoped her companions had such forethought. Gildred had been served lunch and dinner in her apartment, not unusual since she was "in mourning". She ate sparingly from each meal, only the most perishable parts, and saved the rest for her journey. She double-checked everything in the bag, making sure it was all secure and didn't jingle, as well as balanced to hopefully avoid any fatigue from having to carry it. Gildred made sure the grey granite pawn was easily accessible in her belt pouch and took one final look around what she felt was her prison before walking out of her apartment for the last time.

****

Mary and Julie had been friends for almost five years since arriving here in Occursum, both 18 years old then. They started out in the scullery together and worked their way up to hall maids assigned to floors three and four. They one day hoped to be appointed as chamber maids together as well. They were a great team and completed their duties with efficiency. Most of their work was done from ten in the evening to six the following morning when there was very little traffic in the halls.

They had just finished up on the third floor and were going up the steps to the fourth floor when they saw a sister in a red dress coming down the stairs. Tall, thin, with short blond hair, blue eyes, and fair complexion, the Quia was definitely noticeable. They both stood against the railing of the stairs overlooking the Main Gallery below and curtsied for the Sister.

Mary felt it first. Sharp stabbing pain in her back left shoulder travelling down her left arm. Then, sudden stabbing pain in her chest, like her heart was being crushed. Her eyes went wide, and she looked at Julie with a panic, only to see Julie's face mirrored her own. Her vision blurred, and a blackness formed, starting from the outside, growing to the center until all was nothingness.

****

Gildred made her way silently down the Main Gallery stairs as she could. Her bag slung over her left shoulder and her right hand clutching the pawn in her belt pouch, she was ready for any opposition. She heard the foolish maids chattering like a couple of squirrels before she saw them come onto the landing of the third floor. Gildred paused for a moment to see if they would go up or down the stairs. *Down, they live*, she concluded, *up and they die. The foolish maids chose poorly*, she chuckled to herself.

Gildred left the bodies on the landing; she didn't have the time nor the inclination to even hide what she was doing anymore. She would've set the whole place ablaze if she was allowed. *Weak and pathetic fools, the lot of them*, she contemptuously thought.

She made her way across the Main Gallery to one of the many side doors, looking for the one that led to the western stables where she would meet the other three companions.

In the center of the Main Gallery was what many called The Tree of Life. It was an immense Rowan Tree, gifted 1000 years prior by the King of Aquilonem, a long-ago forgotten Kingdom in the North, before the Viventem invasion. Surrounding this vast and towering tree was a low stone wall made from a gleaming white polished marble. On this wall, Gildred failed to notice the two sisters sitting. Instead, she *felt* the Medeis and spun around in surprise to see the weaving of silence that shielded the two sisters from eavesdropping. Of course, they wouldn't have paid Gildred any mind if it wasn't for her sudden turning to face them.

Heflin Quia, of the Green Septem, and Genia Quia, of the Purple Septem, were no strangers to Gildred. Gildred's lip curled up in a snarl, and her eyes narrowed. *Those two!.* Her hand clutched tighter on the pawn. She would go out of her way for those two.

The Medeis popped like a soap bubble as both of their eyes went wide in horror and shock of pain. Gildred ensured that her face was the last one *those two* ever saw. Gildred's face a distorted smile of pleasure in their demise. Those early years of torment, ridicule, and intolerance of her sexuality by *those two*.

Satisfyingly standing over two more corpses, Gildred realized that this pawn was able to not only attack multiple targets simultaneously but also snuff out Medeis like a pin popping a bubble. *A very handy bauble*, she thought as she spun on her heels and hurriedly went through the door leading to the western stables.

She arrived at the stables and met Hamala, Junis, and Kaylee on horseback, leading a fourth horse for her. Gildred mounted the fourth horse, and the four of them rode out of the west gate, over the West Fork bridge, and into Ventus. *FREEDOM AT LAST!* Gildred gleefully thought to herself.

The quartet rode in silence into the better part of the next day, putting as much distance between them and Occursum as they could. Gildred knew that she, at the very least, would be sought after for the funeral arrangements for Carolee. It wouldn't take many dots connecting to four more deaths to point the finger at her, and whoever else had suddenly disappeared. Gildred knew that it would fall on her, so she kept the knowledge of the murders to herself until they reached the first inn they would stay at.

Mostly flat land of large straths of prairie, Ventus wasn't much of a Kingdom in Gildred's eyes. *Pferdeland,* she thought, *Horseland they called it.* Crops didn't grow well in the somewhat arid land, grasses mostly. Perfect for horses and a few cattle. *A poor Kingdom indeed, easily conquered.*

It was a minuscule two-story in height village compared to Occursum. Twelve streets long, bisected by the West Road making a Main Street. The quartet found the only inn quickly, a painted sign of a grazing horse with 'Grazing Inn' underneath. They paid the stable boy with Occursum gold since they were still within a day's hard ride or a two-day leisurely ride from that city of the mighty Spire. Once inside, they secured four separate rooms. Gildred chuckled to herself, *after tonight, they will be more trusting. Once they know that their wagon is hitched to mine.*

They chose a table in the far corner, next to an empty fireplace waiting to be lit when the sun went down. The days were hot and the air dry in Ventus, but the night could be downright chilly. A good 60-degree temperature swing from 110 Fahrenheit in the day to 50 Fahrenheit at night.

Gildred waited for the single serving girl to finish passing out four bowls of stew before she spoke.

"As you know, they will be looking for me and grow suspicious of Carolee's death as a result."

The other three started to eat, as this was obvious to them. Gildred had not taken a spoonful of stew yet and continued to speak.

"What you are unaware of, is that Genia, Heflin, and two hall servants are also dead."

Gildred paused to let the new information sink in. Hamala almost spit a mouthful of stew across the table, Junis started to cough mid-swallow, and Kaylee went as white as her dress. Then, with recognition physically indicated, Gildred pressed on.

"With more *sudden* deaths, comes more suspicion, and a formal rollcall will take place. With you three gone in the same time period as I, you are all as culpable as I."

"We have already sworn allegiance, Gildred!" Hamala quietly protested.

"To him, yes. But not to me, *sister*," Gildred pressed home to Hamala.

"What could you possibly hope to gain from this?" Hamala's knuckles grew white around her spoon.

"Isn't it obvious? Our fates are now tied together." Gildred replied with a chortle. She looked at the other stunned two, satisfied in her plan, and began to eat.

"Where are we going, may I ask?" Kaylee said, finally finding her voice.

"That will be seen in the morning," Gildred replied. "For now, eat and rest up. We leave before daybreak."

They finished their meals, paid the serving girl, and retired to their single rooms on the second floor.

Kaylee closed the door to her room and plopped herself down on the single twin-sized bed made of birch. She held her head in her hands and was about to start questioning where it had all gone wrong. A voice from the opposite corner of the room broke her self-pity.

"Awww, my child. What could ever be so wrong?" the feminine voice mockingly said.

Kaylee shot up off the bed and reached out to Medeis. Shock and fear overcame her, her eyes went wide, as she could feel the power of Medeis, but its sweet taste was just out of reach. *BLOCKED!* She screamed in her head.

"Now, my child," the voice seductively said, "Tell me everything."

Kaylee saw the woman in a shimmering silver dress saunter out of the shadows toward her. She could feel the threads penetrating her mind. Powerless to resist. Frozen in fear.

"Yes, Mistress," was all Kaylee could answer.

"Please, my child," the woman crooned, "Call me Juventus."

Chapter 4

I t was well into the night, and the candles were more than halfway melted to their tin wax catchers. Juventus sat amusedly in a simple roughhewn rustic chair next to a matching side table that doubled as a writing table. Kaylee still stood frozen next to the bed. Her shoulder-length auburn hair matted against her face and neck with profuse sweat. Juventus selected her target, primarily for her height. Dissimulare works best when the height matches. *It's an old trick,* Juventus mused, *but I doubt any of these primitives have worked it out.*

Juventus easily threaded the weave, went through Kaylee's bag, and donned one of her dresses. She turned to Kaylee and stepped toward her. Caressing Kaylee's cheek, she snapped her neck with a flick of her other hand and Medeis. She held Kaylee's body in place with threads of

Air, opened the birch wardrobe, and folded Kaylee's body unnaturally into the closet using Medeis. She closed the wardrobe and wove a trap on the doors. *Curiosity killed the cat*, she laughed.

She looked out the window to check the time. Kaylee said they would be leaving before daybreak. Juventus could see the tiniest of a glow on the eastern horizon. *Perfect timing, as always*, she mused. Picking up Kaylee's bag, she made her way downstairs to the common room, sat at the table in the far corner near the fireplace, and waited for her 'companions'.

Juventus didn't have long to wait, as the other three of the quartet arrived at the table just a few minutes after she did.

"Time to go," Gildred commanded.

The four women made their way to the stables and saddled their horses themselves. The stable boy wouldn't be there for another hour yet. They rode out of the village without seeing another soul. Just the way Gildred wanted it. *No use in leaving breadcrumbs*, she thought.

They rode on the Western Road for the next three days, stopping at small inns similar to the first one, in similar villages. The only difference was that they only paid for two rooms instead of four separate rooms. All part of Gildred's plan of cohesion. On the fourth day, they came to an intersection. The Northern Road went toward the West Fork River and Parva Frater. The Southern Road led to the Ventus capitol city Mächtige Mauer, and beyond to Meridiem.

"We go South," Gildred commanded.

"Sister," Kaylee asked, "What are we looking for in the South?"

Gildred shot Kaylee a disapproving look, but Kaylee only sat high in her horse with that White Septem placidity.

"I suppose I can tell that part now," Gildred reluctantly replied. "There is a young man in a southern border village that can use Medeis. We are to locate him and escort him to the border."

"Does this young man have a name?" Kaylee pressed.

Gildred, becoming disgusted with Kaylee's insolence, was about to berate her and put her in her place, but what came out of her mouth next surprised Junis, Hamala, and even herself.

"His name is Joesiph Williams. He is 6' 1" tall, has shoulder-length brown hair, brown eyes, medium build, and a farmer's tan complexion. He has not yet manifested his power but is on the cusp."

"Ah, thank you, Sister," Kaylee said with a smile and a nod.

Whatever power of information Gildred had, was almost gone in less than 30 seconds. *I still have the pawn,* she thought, *perhaps Kaylee will meet an untimely end if she pries for any more information.*

The quartet turned south onto the Mächtige Mauer Road, Hamala and Junis riding in stunned silence. They had never known Gildred to be so forthcoming with information when simply asked. Nothing was merely given by Gildred. Gildred rode on in disgust at herself and vileness at Kaylee for being able to extract information like taking a small child's hand. Kaylee rode on, sitting high backed in the saddle, looking ahead on the road, and a small, satisfied smile on her face. *Oh,* the disgused Juventus as Kaylee thought, *these truly are simple children.*

The journey south was much the same as the way west had been. Flat, desolate, large stretches of prairie. Scorching hot during the day and chilly at night. The only saving grace was that the air was so dry that any perspiration evaporated as soon as it formed. It was also an extreme danger because dehydration would sneak up and kill the unaware. The quartet made sure they all drank water regularly and filled their waterskins to the brim whenever possible.

On the fourth day on the Mächtige Mauer Road, the quartet had travelled for a total of eight days since leaving Occursum. Gildred had now given Kaylee the Medi Obiectum pawn and told her of the army they were to meet. Gildred, Hamala, and Junis were now very eager to please Kaylee and did *everything* she said. *Yes,* Kaylee amusedly said to herself, *these children need to be led by the hand.*

****

The sun would not rise for another three hours when Genelia woke up Regina.

"How many??" Regina asked again.

"A total of five, counting Carolee," Genelia replied.

"How many know?"

"Three servants and two sisters, Bella and Kiona Quia."

"Send the servants to the Farm. Can the sisters be trusted?"

"I believe the sisters can be trusted, and the servants are already on their way."

"Where are the bodies?"

"I had them placed in the first sub-level."

"Good. Good. Are we sure it's Gildred, Hamala, Junis, and Kaylee?"

"Positive."

"Ugh. They will have at least a day's lead on us. Send the two sisters and make sure they have at least ten Gleidhidh in total."

"As you wish, Mother."

Ugh, Regina thought as she splashed cold water on her face to help wake up; *it's going to be one of those days.*

<u>Chapter 5</u>

Maia Quia was the first to emerge from the portal. Angus, carrying Rowan's unconscious body, followed along with Aislinn, Luigh, and Farr in the rear. They all took in their new surroundings, a steeply sloped land amongst widely spaced short conifers and a few Poplar and Birch trees along with thin cold air; it was apparent to all of them that they were in mountainous terrain. But most of the group didn't know which mountain area they were in, so they all looked to Maia with the same question on their faces.

Maia saw the looks, and before any could ask, looking at Luigh, she said, "It appears we are high in the Western Mountains. We are on the eastern side and most likely near where the Western Mountains meet the Northern Mountains. Gather your wits and strength. We will have a long, arduous journey to the nearest village downslope."

Angus looked flatly at Maia as if something obvious to him she was completely missing. Feeling the frustrated disgust through the Vinculum, she faced him.

"You have something to add, Gleidhidh?" she retorted his look.

Angus merely lifted the still unconscious Rowan in his arms.

"Ahh, yes. This is a good spot to make a quick camp as any. We can start our trek first thing in the morning." Maia then turned to Farr and Damara, "Please see what game you can scare up," then at Luigh and Aislinn, "Gather up sticks and wood for a fire, children. Angus and I will make a shelter."

Luigh narrowed her eyes but kept her mouth shut; accepting orders from Maia was still challenging, but she was making an effort. The rest of the group accepted the directives, as they were keeping in line with what they were all logically thinking.

Farr and Damara shared a smile as they gathered up their bows and quivers. Damara gave Farr a sly wink, and his face beamed back a devilish grin. The game was on, and he was determined to beat her in their ongoing hunting competition.

Aislinn pulled at Luigh's sleeve to get her to start moving into the trees. Luigh, with her back to Maia, began to grumble to herself.

"What?" Aislinn asked Luigh.

"Oh, nothing. I was just talking to myself." Luigh waved a dismissive hand.

"Ohh." Aislinn quietly whispered. *Hopefully, I didn't open a can of worms.* Aislinn winced as she got her answer.

"I mean, seriously! Why are we always on firewood detail!! Rowan is still unconscious!!!" Luigh said with increasing agitation.

Aislinn attempted to console her, "Maia healed him and said his body just needs a little rest. He will be fine and back to his sarcastic self in no time."

"I should be able to do *more* to help him than *she* did!" Luigh almost yelled at Aislinn.

Aislinn recoiled at the ferocity of Luigh's words stopping dead in her tracts, thought for a moment, then realized, "*So you can feel the power difference?*"

Luigh almost tripped on an exposed root at Aislinn's distracting observation.

"I…I suppose I can." Luigh quietly said.

"HAH! *I told you!*" Aislinn said, beaming at being able to prove Luigh wrong.

Luigh narrowed her eyes at Aislinn and balled her fists at her side. Aislinn held up her hands in surrender and laughed. Luigh's shoulders lowered, worked her fingers out of their fists, and shook her head.

"Enjoy it while it lasts," Luigh said with a small smile, and the two of them went into the trees and brush.

At the campsite, Maia used Medeis to neatly gather pine boughs to form a bed that Angus laid Rowan upon. This freed Angus up to make a few lean-tos for the group. He arranged them so the prevailing winds would be against the backside of most of the shelters, and the openings would be toward where the campfire would be.

He was just about done with the shelters when Luigh and Aislinn returned, arms full of wood of various sizes. They dumped them on the ground and arranged a few piles based on the size of the wood. One more trip, and they should have enough to last the night. Even though they were high in the mountains, it was unseasonably still warm for early fall. This fact did not go unnoticed by Maia and Angus.

"The air is off, Maia Quia." Angus stated as fact while he was checking the lashing of the shelters.

"I feel it too," she replied, sitting next to Rowan, "There is a something on the wind, and I fear The Blackness' reach is growing."

"If it is this warm here, there either be banner crops, or the beginning of famine below," Angus said manner-of-factly.

"I fear the latter is more in line with the enemy's plan." Maia dejectedly said.

Angus finished his checks on the shelters, gave a satisfied grunt, and stood over Maia. She was gently stroking Rowan's copper-red hair in a motherly manner.

"What is your plan?" he asked.

She looked up at him, "He needs to grow up faster than he has."

"You need to tell him what that brand means, so he hides it better."

Maia looked at Angus as her eyes widened slightly. *That man does see everything!* she shockingly thought. "When the time is right," she said, looking back at the sleeping young man.

Angus looked flatly at Maia, "We may be past time," and he turned and began to set up the wood for the campfire.

Maia sat there, stopped mid-stroke of Rowan's hair, and blankly stared at her Gleidhidh. *Was it past time? NO! I still have time to prepare them, to prepare him!* She defiantly thought.

Luigh and Aislinn returned with another armful of wood, just as Farr and Damara returned to camp. They held out their arms, showing their bounty of rabbits and wild turkey.

"She beat me again," Farr was telling Luigh and Aislinn as they all walked up to the camp.

"Yes, but you did get more rabbits than I, mo chridhe," Damara said, downplaying his admirations.

"A turkey trumps a few rabbits, love," Farr said with a wink.

"Better than more snake…" Aislinn started to say.

"Start the fire and prepare the food, children." Maia cut her off.

"Yes, Maia Quia," Aislinn said sheepishly like she just got her hand slapped.

"And that brings me to another point, at the Spire, you do not refer to Quia by their names. You will call them, as well as me, Mother. Understood?"

Luigh crossed her arms under her bosom and narrowed her eyes at Maia.

"Now listen here, *Maia Quia*, I have a mother. I may listen and take logical orders from you, but…." Luigh gave a yelp as she was cut off and rubbed at her bottom as if she was smacked.

"I will no longer tolerate back talk. Do you understand??"

Luigh's cheeks colored as she and Aislinn said in unison, "Yes, Mother."

"Good. Now go about your tasks."

"Yes, Mother." They said again, and they quickly lit the campfire with Medeis and went off with Farr and Damara to clean the food.

"A beat dog will bite." Angus quietly said to Maia.

Maia watched the girls go out of earshot, then turned up to Angus.

"I certainly hope so."

There wasn't much conversation that evening, but they did enjoy one of the better meals they had in the wild.

Morning came earlier than most of them wanted. Maia had Angus kick Aislinn and Luigh awake before anyone else had awoken. Giving them orders to make sure the fire was going and breakfast cooking.

Luigh caught Angus' foot on his third attempt to kick her in her ribs.

"If you value your foot, *do not do that ever again*," she coolly warned him.

"I will keep that in mind." He just as coolly responded, but Luigh didn't give his foot back. He pulled at it a few times, then loudly exhaled.

"Do you mind?" he exasperatedly said.

"I do mind."

Angus' eyes narrowed, and he quickly and ruffly pulled his foot free, pulling Luigh a full two feet out of the shelter she was sharing with Aislinn.

"Now, you are up. I suggest you get to work." He said as he walked away.

Aislinn giggled at the exchange, and Luigh, fully prone on her belly, swung her head around like a snake. Aislinn swallowed her laughter. Luigh pushed herself up onto her knees, stood up, and brushed herself off.

"Get up, *child*," Luigh mocked in her best imitation of Maia.

They started the fire and cooked the rest of the rabbits with some sort of root that Damara insisted was similar to potatoes but reminded Aislinn more of turnips. As the group sat back to start eating, they heard a stirring in a shelter.

"What smells good?" Rowan sleepily asked.

"ROWAN!" Aislinn shouted as she bolted up and ran to him, almost crushing him where he lay.

"Umph! ER, ummm, I c…t br..the!" he tried to say.

Aislinn got off him, "What??"

"I said, I can't breathe," he laughed.

Aislinn sat back on her heels and laughed with him.

"Well, you gave us all quite a scare, bulkhead."

"Everyone?"

"Well, everyone but Maia. She said you'd be ok."

"Mr. Mountain??" Rowan incredulously asked.

"He carried you like his own baby!" Aislinn said.

"Whoa," Rowan said in awe, looking at the big man in a different light.

"Come eat, whelp," Angus commanded Rowan.

"Well, that didn't last long," Rowan said to Aislinn as he shrugged his shoulders. Aislinn smiled at Rowan and tussled his hair. The pair got up and made their way to the campfire to join the others at breakfast. Rowan desperately tried to fill a cavernous hole in his stomach and consumed three whole rabbits, six potato/turnip roots, and all of the left-over turkey.

"Would you like the kitchen sink too?" asked Luigh in disgust.

"Sorry," Rowan responded, "I don't know what got into me. Once I started, I couldn't stop."

"That would be the after effect of *Healing*," Maia told them. "The more Healing that is done, the more ravenous the patient will be."

Rowan looked down at his right palm, no longer searing with the pain he remembered. He undid the loose bandages and saw it. The Celtic, runic bird, branded in the center of his right palm. He slowly closed his right hand into a fist and closed his eyes. *The duel with Aeneas, an Adversus. A long-ago forgotten male wielder of Medeis that had been trapped in some sort of Void. Maia had said that the Void was a space between this plane and another. Aeneas bested the whole group easily, and almost killed me, but he said I was to be taken alive. Where? And Why?* Rowan reflected. He opened his eyes to find everyone was looking at him. Luigh, Aislinn, and Farr with sympathy, and Damara with curiosity. Maia and Angus looked at him like an adder, wondering when he would strike. This newfound look took Rowan aback, but before he could recoil, Maia said, "I suggest you keep that covered…to protect the wound."

"Here, boy," Angus said as he threw a pair of jet-black leather gloves at Rowan.

Rowan caught the gloves and slowly pulled them on. They were tight but fit well enough.

"Time to break camp," Maia announced.

Luigh and Aislinn doused and buried the campfire while Angus and Rowan dismantled the shelters. Farr and Damara were sent to refill the waterskins at a nearby stream they found while Maia orchestrated the whole affair.

"Southeast." Maia pointed to Angus. The big man took a step forward, then turned around and walked up to Rowan in a very determined way. Upon seeing Angus' determination, Rowan almost took a fighting stance as he only saw the man do this towards what was a perceived threat.

Angus took off a third sword belt that Rowan had failed to notice the man was wearing. Angus held it out for Rowan to take.

"I rewrapped the hilt." Angus gruffly said.

Rowan straightened up and let out a held breath.

"Um, thanks?" Rowan sheepishly said as he took the sword and belted it on. Angus grunted in reply and trod off in the Southeast direction Maia wanted.

The group instinctively fell into their usual marching order. Angus scouting ahead, Maia, then Luigh, Aislinn, Damara, Farr, and Rowan bringing up the rear.

Chapter 6

T he salty air was hot and oppressively humid. He felt like taking another bath, even though all he had done was put on clothes after just taking one. *How do they tolerate this heat and humidity?* he contemptibly thought. *It's so uncivilized!* He embraced Medeis, grabbed hold of the Power, and did a simple weave around his skin. "Ahhh, much better," he said to the empty room. *No need to suffer like I will make these primitives suffer,* he sneered in thought. He finished getting dressed by strategically hiding a couple of daggers and belting on two long blades on each side of his waist. He was never any good with a sword, and they didn't have any projectile weapons in this time. He looked at himself in the tall mirror in the room. *Good enough for any royal court these days,* he mused. At 5 feet 4 inches, he wasn't very tall by any standard. His short black hair and neatly trimmed black goatee, dark brown eyes, and light olive tan complexion, allowed him to blend into almost any southern location to the point that he was constantly overlooked. Just the way he liked it, not be seen, but seeing everything. *Knowledge is Power,* he chuckled at the old thought. Vermi took one last look at his black flowing silk shirt and matching pants in the mirror. *Yes,* he said to himself, *good enough.* He tied off the weave keeping him cool and less humid, and released Medeis. Vermi opened the door of his room and made his way down the hall of the Grand Palace of Meridiem.

The Grand Palace almost reminded Vermi of a hotel he frequently attended back in his youth. Large arches along the hallway with white marble columns. Some of the archways were open to large plazas with fountains, white marble statues meticulously anatomically carved, or some sort of olive tree. The Palace itself was straightforward to navigate as it was a giant square, with many little squares therein. It rose a total of only six stories, with the Royal family occupying the top floor, visiting dignitaries on the fourth and fifth floors, the third floor was administrative and Royal library, and the bottom two floors were mainly open to the sky, except for the central square. That was the Grand Royal Hall, and that was where Vermi was headed. The whole Palace sprawled across nine square blocks in the center of the port city known as Fairharbour, Capitol of Meridiem.

Vermi didn't see much of the city in the past week since he had arrived here by Itinerantur. He had luckily opened a portal in the back of a clothing shopkeeper, who became most agreeable after using Coacta on the shopkeeper. What he did see of the city was a very organized grid of city blocks, all the same, gleaming white marble colonnaded square buildings taking up most of the block, with various shops divided in the large central building. All neat and very organized. *Easy to navigate and even easier to control,* Vermi thought.

He made his way to a side entrance of the Grand Hall, and the guard in red livery with a golden lion on his chest opened the door for Vermi. *It has been oh too easy to be ingrained here,* Vermi snickered as he strode through the doorway. Making his way up to the dais, he paused for a brief second to take in who was around.

King George IX of Estinhouse was seated on the dais, the Captain of the Guard was to his left, and a local Nobleman was currently in audience. The Captain of the Guard was of no consequence to Vermi, so he never learned the man's name, but the King, that, was his target. A portly man in his early fifties, completely bald, a neatly trimmed grey goatee as was the fashion he had started. He was dressed in a red silk shirt with a golden lion on his chest with black silk billowing pants. Like most inhabitants of this area, the King sweated profusely but somehow ignored that fact by dousing himself with perfumes and scented powders.

Vermi, after taking stock of the situation, seized Medeis. The Power surged in him, threatened to consume him with fire, and burn him to ash. He relished in it and grabbed control. Vermi reached out with it and, with almost imperceptible whisps, did the delicate weaving needed for Coacta to properly work. If done crudely, the target would be lobotomized or worse. It was a very delicate art, which took a lot of skill and patience. Not many Adversus were able to do it. It was what he thought of as his edge. Vermi knew he was the weakest of all of them, but his ability and deftness to blend in and obtain knowledge was his gift.

He was contemptuous of this current assignment but grateful to be finally out in the world. Vermi also took great pride in his work, even if the task was as menial as he felt this one was. Satisfied that the weaving was complete, he neatly tied it off, confidently strode up to the dais, addressed the King, and cut off the Nobleman in mid-sentence.

"…in the Eastern half of the crops…"

"My Liege," Vermi began, "I have some urgent business to discuss."

The King held up a hand to the Nobleman, "Leave us."

The Nobleman bowed his head toward the King and shot Vermi a look of disgust for being so rudely interrupted as he stormed off.

Vermi ignored the insignificant man and addressed the King, "In private, my Liege."

King George gave a dismissive wave of his hand, emptying the room.

"Go on." The King commanded.

"My Liege, there is an urgent opportunity to the North that I think the Kingdom would benefit from. The crops here have been poor this summer, but they are more plentiful in Ventus. That Kingdom is vast, and the southern border is weakly defended. We should annex more land to fulfill the needs of your people."

"What do you propose?"

"Give me 2000 troops under my command. I will not only secure more land for crops, but I will bend Ventus to your will."

"Hmmm," the King thought aloud, "my people do need the food. Do this in my name!"

"As you command, my Liege." Vermi said with an oily smile. "Have the troops ready tomorrow. I will meet them at the North Gate."

"Agreed," replied King George IX.

Vermi gave the curtest of nods to the King and strode back to his room as confidently as he strode in. *All too easy,* he chuckled to himself.

The next morning, Vermi met the 2nd and 3rd calvary divisions at the North Gate. The Captain of the 2nd was a tall skinny man by the name of Dennis Faust, and the Captain of the 3rd was a man of medium height and build by the name of Francis Kilroy. Neither were of any merit to Vermi past the need to pass on his commands. The Captains rode up to meet Vermi, their bannermen shadowing them with red banners fringed with gold and a gold lion in the center.

"What are your orders, Sir?" Faust asked Vermi.

"We ride North to Ventus." Vermi replied.

"By your command, Sir." They said in unison and rode back to their respective units to relay the order.

They rode out in two massive groups of four columns wide, with 1000 horsemen in each group. The 2nd division in the lead with Vermi in the center, Faust to his Left, Kilroy to his right, and a bannerman flanking the two captains on the outside. *An impressive invasion force in this era,* Vermi thought.

The small army of calvary rode painfully slow for Vermi, despite Faust and Kilroy's insistence and pride that they were making good time. It had been almost a whole week since they left Fairharbour, and Vermi was told the Ventus border was just a short two more weeks away. Vermi wanted to wring their necks every time they gave him the evening and morning updates. Vermi was a patient man, but patience has its limits. Aries was emphatic in the last "dream" that Vermi was to not use Medeis in any outward fashion until Joesiph was secured. *Ugh,* Vermi moaned to himself, *I could portal us there in minutes; even a ho-car was faster!*

"What's a hocar?" Kilroy asked Vermi.

"A what?" Vermi said, shocked and startled out of his thoughts.

"You mumbled something about a *hocar* was faster."

Vermi blankly started back at Kilroy as he scrambled to cover his gaffe. "I didn't realize I was thinking out loud, but what I meant was a horse cart was faster."

"True," Faust responded, "but an army must retain the semblance of organization."

Kilroy nodded in agreement, but Vermi just sighed in silent resignation. *Two more painfully slow weeks with these insufferable fools*, Vermi thought, making sure he didn't mumble this time.

Chapter 7

The morning sun would rise in the east in the next hour or so, the orange glow low on the horizon pushing back the black stary night to the west. The air was crisp but not as cold as when Juventus had assumed the identity of Kaylee two weeks prior. She knew the day would be oppressively hot, and the humidity was beginning to increase in the air. Not swampy-humid, but not as arid as it had been. Juventus had already washed up and weaved a protective layer against the sun's rays to protect her skin and keep her cool. She donned one of Kaylee's white dresses and packed up her bag. Juventus knew everything these "Quia" knew about their mission and had them tightly wrapped with Coacta and didn't care to fold her weaves, except Dissimulare. She was better at it than almost all of the other Adversus, save Vermi, but never let on how good she was at it. In fact, there was only one other person who knew her true abilities, and he was long dead. Juventus let out a long sigh at the memory of her lost love. She shook herself out of her reminiscence. *I have a second chance now*, she smiled as she thought, *with him*. She closed up her travel bag, slung it over her left shoulder, and made her way down into the common room for breakfast.

Juventus had just finished her meal of some poached eggs and sausage she was not entirely sure was from a pig. As she sipped her tea, her companions made their way to the table, a few minutes separating each arrival.

"Good morning." Juventus beamed at them when they were all seated.

"Good morning, Kaylee!" they all beamed back in unison. The eagerness to please Juventus had them all jittering in their seats. Juventus giggled to herself.

"How much further, Gildred?" Juventus asked.

"I estimate one more full day of riding should bring us to the farmstead. I suggest we ride the outskirts of the village to avoid prying eyes." Gildred enthusiastically responded.

Juventus knew the next village was their first destination, and the Ventus/Meridiem border was the second, but she didn't know the exact lay of the land like these primitives did. For now, she allowed Gildred to feel like she still had some semblance of leadership; otherwise, the Coacta would not have been as effective. The other two minds were as pliable as warm clay. *How useful they don't know the protection weave*, she thought as she smiled at them.

"I suggest you all eat heartily then," Juventus said.

"Great idea!" they all beamed back.

Juventus sat back with her tea and waited for the others to finish their breakfast.

When they had finished up in the common room, the quartet made their way out the back door leading to the inn's stables. Gildred paid the stable boy, as Juventus had suggested Gildred do all the paying with Occursum gold, knowing full well it would leave a trail of breadcrumbs. Juventus estimated that whomever they send from Occursum would be at most three to four days behind them. Enough time to find out who this group is meeting and why, and it offers a way of a diversion to slip away when they get caught. *Another benefit of these ignorant Quia is that they can't Iter,* she mused.

Gildred led the quartet southbound out of the village, with Juventus second, Hamala third, and Junis last. They rode their horses alternating from a walk to a fast trot, stopping at midday to stretch their own legs and eat. Juventus suggested that Hamala and Junis care for all the horses before they continued on. The pair eagerly jumped to it, pleased that Kaylee spoke to them.

"Gildred?" Juventus asked.

"Yes?"

"I suggest that I handle the young boy, Joesiph, was it?"

"Yes, Joesiph Williams. As you wish, sister." Gildred acquiesced.

"Excellent." Juventus smiled.

They rode on doing the quick long ride of the horses as they had been to optimize their time. It was a very sore affair on one's tailbone the first few days Juventus did that, but she had gotten used to it and was also starting to like the control riding a horse gave her. *It's not as fast and easy as Iter, but it's more enjoyable than a ho-car.* They arrived around dusk at what Gildred claimed to be Williams' farmstead.

"You three wait here," Juventus told them. "I'll be back in a moment."

The three Black Quia nodded with eager smiles that creepily split their faces.

Juventus dismounted her horse, stretched out her back a little, smoothed her dress, and strode to the front door. She knocked on it three times before it was finally answered by an older man in his early fifties. He opened his mouth to say something, but his eyes went wide as he was lifted into the air, his arms tight against his sides. Juventus coolly held him with Medeis in front of her as she made her way into the farmhouse.

As she walked from the living room into a small hallway that led to the kitchen, she admired how simple the furnishings were. A woman was at the woodstove in the kitchen, and a young man was setting the table for dinner. Juventus deftly wove threads or air around both of them, and they hung paralyzed inches off the ground. She used Medeis to maneuver the old man next to the other two.

"Now, before I release the gags and allow you to speak," Juventus started, "I first need you to listen."

Juventus looked at them and waited until she saw acknowledgment in their eyes.

"Good," she continued, "I am Kaylee Quia. I have ridden fast from Occursum with three other sisters for you, Joesiph. You will soon manifest the power of Medeis, if you haven't already. There is another group of sisters coming a few days behind us. They will not be as nice as I am. They will cut you off from Medeis, which I hear is a fate worse than death. If you willingly and quietly come with me, I will help you. Blink once if you agree."

Joesiph made an overly exaggerated single blink.

"Ahh, very good." Juventus smiled and released them. "What's for dinner?"

"Just a simple stew, mistress." Joesiph's mother said as she gave her best clumsy curtsy.

"That sounds yummy," Juventus said, "and please, call me Kaylee." She turned to Joesiph's father and said, "Please go out and invite my sisters to join us for dinner."

"As you wish, mistress Kaylee." He shakenly said as he knuckled his forehead in a salute and hastily made his way out the front door to the three awaiting Quia.

The seven of them finished dinner with no conversation, Joesiph and his parents in fear and awe that four Quia were in their humble farmhouse.

"Sister Junis, would you escort Joesiph to his room to gather his things to go with us?" Juventus said to Junis.

"It would be my pleasure, sister Kaylee." She replied with a big smile.

"Oh, before I forget," Juventus said to Joesiph as she wove the shield around him and tried it off, "best not to have you do anything rash just yet."

Joesiph's eyes went wide as he exhaled and doubled over as if he was just gut-punched.

"Wha? What did you do?!?" he exclaimed when he caught his breath.

"I temporarily shielded you from Medeis until I can teach you how to control it. Now go with sister Junis please." Juventus calmly said.

"Yes, mistress Kaylee." Joesiph dejectedly replied.

Junis and Joesiph were gone for about five minutes when they returned, ready to leave.

"Oh, good." Juventus crooned. "That was fast. Master Williams, would you saddle a horse and bring it around front for Joesiph? And Mrs. Williams, would you pack up some sturdy travelling fare for us?"

Mr. Williams got up from the table and went out the back door while Mrs. Williams started to pack some cheeses, loaves of bread, and dried meats. She gave the food to Joesiph in an oiled and waterproofed bag that could easily be tied to a horse's saddle.

"Say goodbye, Joesiph," Juventus told him, and he hugged his mother goodbye.

Juventus got up from the table and led the group out the front door to their horses. Mr. Williams was there with a horse for Joesiph.

"Thank you, Mr. Williams," Juventus said to the middle-aged man. Joesiph shook his father's hand, and they both nodded at each other.

"Be ready to ride, Joesiph. I want a moment alone with your parents." Juventus told him.

Joesiph tied the food bag on his horse's saddle and mounted it. The other three Quia also climbed on their horses as Juventus returned to the house with Mr. Williams.

She was in the farmhouse for less than five minutes when she came sauntering out of the front door, not even bothering to close it, a smile on her face, and her left hand in her belt pouch grasping a grey granite smooth chess pawn.

"Time to go." She announced to the group. "Sister Gildred, would you be so kind as to lead us to our next destination?"

"Yes, Sister Kaylee, I would love to!" Gildred replied with that creepy smile as she kicked her heels into her horse and made her way south to the Meridiem border.

They travelled for another two days until they reached the last village in Ventus. They stayed at the only Inn and left at daybreak, riding only a few hours when they saw a big cloud of dust in the distance to the south on the road.

"Our final destination." Gildred excitedly said to Juventus, hoping she would be pleased.

They slowed their horses to a casual trot and allowed the host causing the dust to come to them.

As the calvary army came into view, Juventus could see the two red banners fringed with gold and a golden lion in the center. As the army got closer, she could see the little man in the front and center.

No! It can't be! Juventus wildly thought, *THAT WEASEL!!*

Chapter 8

The way down the mountain was strenuous. They had to crisscross several times due to drop-offs, rivers, and gorges. The forest grew denser with deciduous oak, maple, sumac, and chestnut trees. The underbrush was occasionally thick with thorny briars that sometimes forced the group to extensive waterways and ravines.

Angus instructed and warned the crew of the Novus about some of the poisonous plants and vines like poison ivy, poison oak, and poison sumac. Unfortunately for Rowan, this instruction came a day late, after he used a poison ivy leaf to clean after relieving himself. Aislinn, Leigh, and Damara had a good laugh about how he kept trying to scratch himself through his pants before Maia healed him.

It took the group eight days to get down the mountain before seeing the first signs of so-called civilization. There were a few thin whisps of grey smoke from a couple of chimneys in the village. As before, Maia instructed them to let her do the talking and not use any names until she said they could.

They made their way down into the small village and to the only Inn at the center of town. The sign above the doorway had a picture of a snowcapped crowned mountain with the words underneath "Storm King's Rest".

Maia led them into the Inn and pointed to a table in the far corner with one of two maple tables that could seat eight. The Inn itself was unremarkable and simple with a cobblestone first floor and the second story of wood. The furnishings appeared to be all made of maple. But after roughing it for almost the past three weeks, it was first class to them. The Innkeeper was a gruffly stoic, fit man that reminded Rowan of the men he had seen in Parva Frater. The sides of his head were shaved, and the top pulled back into a ponytail. If it wasn't for the white telltale Innkeeper apron, Rowan thought the man could be a soldier at Das Daingneach.

"Ah, Hail Mistress Quia! Hail Master Gleidhidh! I'm Master Innes, Innkeeper." Innes came from around the front bar area to greet Maia and Angus. *Well*, Rowan thought, *no pretenses here.*

"Hail and well met, Master Innes," Maia said. "We will require two adjoining rooms and direction to where we can acquire some horses."

"Ah, well and good. I will have your rooms ready by the time your bellies are full. As to horses, you'll find Master Blacksmith McTavish two buildings down and across the main square. Let him know I sent you." Innes said with a wink.

"I thank you, Master Innkeeper Innes," Maia said as she inclined her head to him.

Inness beamed a smile at the intonation and made a sweeping motion with his arm as he moved back to allow them to pass into the common room.

Maia led the group over to the table she had pointed out.

As they sat down, Rowan blurted out, "Well, I guess there's no hiding her..."

The dead look of daggers from Angus stopped Rowan in mid-word.

Maia quietly said, "As Rowan so observantly pointed out, we are somewhat recognized, but not fully. For now, I am Mary, and Angus is Andrew. You all will remain in our rooms while Angus and Rowan get horses after dinner. Farr, Damara, for now, we will split the rooms by gender. Be vigilant, The Blackness is still searching for us." She looked at Rowan at that last bit. He swallowed hard as her gaze fell on him and hung his head down, ashamed that he was still acting like a child when he knew better by now. *I'm the one it wants. No one is safe around me. I can't sneak away here; besides, where can I go??.*

Rowan was still lost in his melancholy self-loathing that he didn't even notice the steak, green beans, and mashed potatoes in front of him.

"Rowan?" Aislinn sheepishly asked with concern, "You ok??"

"Wha?" He asked as he shook his head. Snapping out of his thoughts and noticed the food in front of him. He looked up and saw that almost everyone was looking at him. Aislinn, Leigh, Damara, and Farr had looks of concern. Angus was scowling at him like a father about to trounce his kid for back talking. Maia appeared to be the only one ignoring him as she daintily cut her steak, her back straight in the chair, and ate as if she were dining with a King. "Oh, I'm fine. Just lost in thought. Boy, am I starving!" He said with a forced smile, holding his knife in one hand and a fork in the other. As he started to eat, the others watched him as he took his first bite and then ate themselves. They kept the conversation to a minimum during their meal. Innes came over when he saw they were finished.

"I'll show you to your rooms, Mistress Quia."

"Thank you, Master Innkeeper Innes. The meal was excellent."

Maia left a few gold coins on the table, and Inness beamed at her.

"If you would please follow me." He said and started off toward the stairs in the center of the building by the front bar.

He led them up the stairs, turned left, went all the way to the end of the hall, and pointed to the last two rooms on the left. There were stairs across the hall that led back down, presumably to a back door and kitchen area.

"Please don't hesitate to let me know if you need anything else, Mistress Quia."

"I thank you, Master Innkeeper Innes," Maia replied.

Innes inclined his head at her and made off down the back stairs.

Maia didn't need to give any instructions here. The group split by gender to their respective rooms.

Angus and Rowan put their stuff on the two simple maple twin beds, while Farr put his on the small maple writing table by the window.

"Come, boy," Angus commanded.

Rowan looked at Farr, who was smiling and putting up his hands, indicating that he was not being spoken to. Rowan rolled his eyes, sighed, put on a fake smile, and spun on his heels toward Angus.

"Lead on." Rowan intoned.

Angus arched an eyebrow at Rowan and fought the urge to pounce. Instead, he gave a low growl and walked out of the room. Rowan turned back and winked at Farr, who shook his head and smiled. Rowan followed Mr. Mountain out of the room, down the main stairs, and out of the Inn toward Master Blacksmith McTavish's.

Chapter 9

Maia and the girls made their way into their room. Maia put her stuff on one of the simple maple twin beds and looked at Damara.

Damara knew what Maia was about to say, "Oh, don't worry about me, Maia Quia. I'll take the floor."

Maia smiled at Damara and said, "As you wish, but please take some bedding."

Maia held out one of the two down pillows. Damara took it and the spare blanket at the foot of the bed. Aislinn quickly saw this and handed Damara the blanket from her bed as well.

"Thanks." Damara said as she smiled at Aislinn.

"Before we all get settled in, there is training we must do, children," Maia said to them. "I need a volunteer to get a small cut."

All three of them looked back and forth until Luigh finally let out an exasperated "Fine! I'll do it," as she shot daggers at Aislinn and Damara.

"Good. But Damara stepped up first." Maia announced.

Luigh was taken aback, Aislinn was shocked, but Damara simply stepped forward as if she volunteered all along.

Luigh was about to protest, but a stern look from Maia stifled it quickly.

"Please hold out your hand," Maia said to Damara, who complied.

Maia took Damara's hand in her left hand, held a small knife in her right hand above Damara's palm, and looked at Aislinn and Luigh. "Pay close attention to the weaves."

Maia quickly ran the edge of the blade along Damara's palm, exerting a small amount of pressure to thinly slice the skin, and a small trickle of red blood began to pool along the length of the cut. Damara winced but did not pull her hand away. Maia released Damara's hand and put the knife away. Aislinn and Luigh saw the glow of Medeis spring forth around Maia, and then the strands began to form.

Luigh and Aislinn saw the thick strands of Air and Water separate as they were split again and again into thin whisps of threads. They watched in awe as the threads were woven back and forth in an alternating, even pattern between Maia's outheld hands. The weave formed a small patchwork. Maia moved her hands to Damara's still outheld cut hand, the Medeis patchwork moving with Maia's hands. As Maia touched Damara's hand, the Medeis patchwork seemed to be absorbed into Damara's palm, with a thin thread coming out each side of Damara's hand. Maia moved her hands to each thread and pulled. Damara gave a slight shiver as the cut was pulled shut. Maia smiled at Damara and motioned to the maple side table with a porcelain pitcher and basin. Damara understood and went over to it and washed her hands.

Maia turned toward Luigh and Aislinn. "Did you see?" she asked.

"Yes, Mother." They both said in unison.

"Good. Aislinn, you are next."

Aislinn wanted to give a small squeal of excitement but was hesitant because she didn't want to hurt her friend.

Maia took notice of Aislinn's hesitation.

"You saw the pattern?"

"Yes, Mother."

"Then do not worry. Do it exactly as I have shown you."

"Yes, Mother."

Damara returned to where she had initially stood and held out her palm. Maia cut it ever so slightly again. The glow of Medeis sprang up around Aislinn, and she held her hands up to her eye level, palms facing each other about a foot apart, and began to copy the pattern of Medeis patchwork that Maia had done previously. Luigh watched Aislinn copy it precisely as Maia, and then it came to her in a flash. Combine her knowledge of anatomy with Medeis. She was now eager for her turn.

Damara washed off the clotting blood from her second healed cut and retook her position for Luigh's turn.

"You know the pattern?"

"Oh, yes, Mother."

Maia cocked an eyebrow at Luigh's enthusiasm.

"I got this," Luigh assured her with a sly wink.

"Then begin, child," Maia said as she gave Damara another precise small cut on her palm.

The glow of Medeis sprang up quickly and brighter around Luigh than it did for Aislinn and even Maia. So much so that Maia's eyes widened in surprise, and she almost was ready to shield Luigh.

"No! Mother." Luigh said in calm focus, "I have it under control."

Maia stopped her shield pattern but held on to Medeis. Aislinn looked from Luigh to Maia and back to Luigh in wonder.

Luigh looked at Damara's palm and made deft movements in the air above the wound but didn't touch her. Damara gave a shiver as the cut closed.

"Where did you….How did you….??" Maia asked quizzically.

"Biology 101." Luigh answered with a sly smile before adding, "Mother."

Aislinn gave out a guffawed, "Of course!" as she slapped her forehead.

"What is…Biology 101?" Maia asked, confused.

"It's the study of life, beginner level." Luigh chided.

Maia, unamused, put her hands on her hips and stared at Luigh.

Luigh realized that she may have pushed too far with her sarcasm.

"Sorry, Mother."

"You will teach me this……Biology 101, child."

"Yes, Mother."

"But," Maia said, "for now, we should rest. We will get our true bearings in the morning and figure out how far we are from Occursum."

"Yes, Mother." Luigh and Aislinn both said in unison.

"I saw there was a room with two baths by the main stairs," Aislinn said to Luigh. "May we, Mother?" she directed at Maia.

"Stay together."

"Yes, Mother."

Aislinn and Luigh gathered up their spare, clean clothes joined arms to walk to the baths when they suddenly realized that they couldn't fit through the door in such a manner. They let go of their intertwined arms and laughed all the way down the hallway. Damara shook her head at their adolescent behavior and made her bed on the floor.

Aislinn and Luigh were neck-deep in their separate tubs, having made the water tepid enough with a quick shot of Medeis.

"I saw it, you know." Aislinn started.

"Saw what? My weaving?" Luigh asked.

"Well, yeah, that was ingenious, by the way. I should have thought about that, being the medic and all, but that's not what I meant. I saw your glow and Maia's." Aislinn stated.

"So??" Luigh said sarcastically.

"So! Your glow of Medeis was like an SDL drive at full burn compared to a matchstick!!!" Aislinn exclaimed as she quickly moved to the side of the tub near Luigh's tub, causing some water and bubbles to splash over the side and onto the floor.

"Really?" Luigh said incredulously.

"Totally!! I told you, we are more powerful than she is." Aislinn said smugly.

"But, Maia knows more." Luigh admonished.

"Yeah, yeah. I'm not saying she's holding us back, but whatever we do learn, we can do with more power." Aislinn retorted.

"Want to know the scary part??" Luigh quietly said, peering over the side of the tub at Aislinn.

"What?" Aislinn asked. Her curiosity peeked.

"I could do more……a lot more." Luigh breathlessly said.

"Whoa," Aislinn said, astonished as she sank back in her tub.

The pair sat there a while in contemplative silence.

Luigh broke the silence first. "I bet there's a lot more we could do than these other Quia if we applied our advanced knowledge of science and technology to Medeis."

"Maybe." Aislinn thought, "but, that could be dangerous also. Remember what Maia said 'Some Quia burned out or worse' trying new patterns."

"True, but if we use an already existing pattern and either make it more efficient or expand on it, I don't see the harm." Luigh smugly said.

"I dunno, Luigh. Maybe." Aislinn said, concerned.

"Forget it for now. Let's wash up." Luigh said, trying to assuage her worry.

They finished washing up, dried off, and redressed in clean clothes. They then did their best to wash their dirty clothes in the bath and wrung them out before heading back to their room.

As they returned to their room, they ran into Angus and Rowan.

"How'd ya make out?" Aislinn asked Rowan.

Rowan put his finger to his lips and slightly shook his head no. The four of them walked into the room; well, Luigh, Aislinn, and Rowan walked. Angus marched in. If Maia hadn't opened the door at the right moment, Rowan thought that Angus would've walked right through the door.

"Problem?" Maia cooed at Angus. She already knew his frustration and anger through the Vinculum.

Angus scowled at her and growled in a low baritone, gravelly voice, "He would only sell us five horses."

"Not to worry, my Gleidhidh," Maia said soothingly in voice and along the Vinculum as well. Angus' face softened as well as stone can be said to soften, but he did take in a deep breath and let it out.

"I will ask Master Innkeeper Innes in the morning if there is anything he can do to help us. If not, Rowan and Farr can ride double, and Aislinn and Luigh can ride double. Plan b." Maia said to him and smiled a soft smile.

"As you wish, Maia Quia." Angus said to her. As he turned and started to walk out of the room, he boomed at Rowan, "Come, boy!"

Rowan shrugged his shoulders at the girls and followed Angus out of the room.

Rowan was about to go into his room instinctually, but Mr. Mountain had other ideas. Angus walked right past the door and went down the back stairs. *Ugh*, Rowan moaned in his head, *more training!*

The following day, Rowan woke with aching muscles that he didn't get to exercise for the past week. The woods coming down the mountain became too thick to practice. He wasn't as sore as when he was in the Keep, but stiff, nonetheless. He was also severely bruised, as he was highly distracted in his own thoughts. He had to figure something out, and soon, that would keep him from putting his friends in danger. *I'm the target*, he thought over and over, *I'm who The Blackness wants*. But the answer of what to do kept eluding him.

He sat up in bed and saw that Farr was already washed up and ready to go down to breakfast. With a groan, Rowan rolled out of his bed and made his way over to the pitcher and wash basin. He looked over at Angus' bed and saw that it was empty.

"Go on ahead, Farr." Rowan said, "I'll be right down."

"You sure?" Farr asked.

"Yup. I'll be quick." Rowan assured him.

"Ok," Farr replied and went down to meet the others in the common room.

Rowan splashed the cold water on his face and the back of his neck. The chilly water made him shiver. He used the bar of soap in the basin and lathered up his hands, neck, and face, then rinsed. He toweled off and made his way down to the common room, longingly glancing at the room with the two baths before heading down the stairs.

As he approached the table, he noticed that his food was already waiting, and the others had just started to eat.

"See?" he told Farr, "Told you I wouldn't miss breakfast."

Farr chuckled and smiled around a slice of apple.

After the group had finished eating, Maia announced to the table, "Master Innkeeper Innes has graciously given us one more horse. That's good news for Aislinn and Luigh, but I'm afraid Rowan and Farr will still have to ride double. We will need the last horse for a pack animal. If there is room, I think you may be light enough to ride it if you wish, Farr."

"Thank you,' Farr replied and looked at Rowan, who winked at him, "but I think I'll still ride double with Rowan."

"As you wish," Maia said. "I was also able to learn that we are almost where I had thought. We are in Parva Frater, but a little further Northwest than I had thought. We have two choices. Go East to Das Daingneach, then South again on our original path to Occursum, or South from here into Ventus, then East to Occursum. We don't have to decide right now. The next village to our south will be the crossroads for that to happen."

Angus stood up and looked at Rowan, "Come, whelp."

Ugh, Rowan thought, *I'm back to whelp after last night's crappy practice. Oh well.* Rowan got up and followed Angus past the main stairs and front bar, past the kitchen and back stairs, and out the back door to the stables.

"We should go too," Maia said to the rest of the group as she pushed away from the table and stood. Maia placed a small pile of gold coins on the table, went over to Innes, and pressed a few gold coins in his hand as she thanked him for his hospitality. Innes beamed at her, said it was his pleasure, and hoped she would return. Maia smiled at him, and the group continued on to the back door toward the stables.

Chapter 10

T he group rode through the remote Northwest Parva Frater village, heading South by Southeast to the next village where they would choose to go either East or South.

The day started off as a cool early Autumn Day, but the hazy rising sun threatened to quickly reach mid-summer temperatures as if the world was two months behind. The grasses were yellowing to a golden brown, baking in the harsh sun, and the ground was dry and packed hard with small cracks showing a lack of moisture. Many animals took advantage of the cooler weather in the early hours, but most would soon find refuge in yellowing underbrush, leaving insects to be the dominant noisy nuisance. For this very reason, the group kept their sleeves rolled down for most of the day, and Rowan kept his light cloak hood up over his head to help protect from the blood-sucking small flying insects Angus called midges. Aislinn, Luigh, Maia, and Farr didn't seem to have a problem with the midges, *probably because they are all short,* Rowan grumbled under his pulled-down hood. Damara's light but thick hair offered her protection, and Angus was either immune or didn't care about the minuscule hordes of flying vampires.

The high-pitched and growing intensity of buzzing from cicadas announced another hot day as Aislinn and Luigh rode next to each other.

"….so, picture the double lipid membrane, with the receptor proteins on each lipid," Luigh continued to lecture Aislinn.

"Yeah," replied Aislinn.

"Now the cytoplasmic fluid, with di-lipid vacuoles, proteins, all leading to the endoplasmic reticulum." Luigh continued.

"Ok," Aislinn said. Neither of them noticed that Maia had slowed down her horse to get closer and listen in.

"Now, see that everything isn't totally just floating about, but connected by Intermediate Filaments to form a cytoskeleton and transport system," Luigh explained.

"Oh yeah!" Aislinn agreed.

"I figure that if you can get Water, Fire, and Air thin enough, you can stimulate enzymatic reactions, protein production, and even nuclear articulation, such as RNA and DNA transcription and translation." Luigh postulated.

"Whoa," Aislinn said in a hushed tone of wonderment.

"Right?! And don't get me started on the cytokine and immune responses! The applications are making my mind race!!" Luigh said in a rush of excitement.

"I may have been the cursory medic, but I think you missed your true calling," Aislinn told Luigh, slowly shaking her head in amazement.

"Oh? What's that??" Luigh asked quizzically.

"You should've been a doctor!" Aislinn exclaimed with a big smile, and the two laughed as Luigh gave Aislinn a dismissive wave of her hand.

"I dunno, Biology, and Botany came easily in college and Grad school, but the opportunity at the Academy was too good to pass up," Luigh said, "but, I did think about Med-school prior to that."

"Even though I did not understand most of the words," Maia interrupted, "I do recognize that you should keep this *knowledge* to yourselves for now."

Luigh and Aislinn shot straight up in their saddles, startled at how Maia seemed to teleport from leading the pack to right next to them, horse and all.

Maia continued, "Most Yellows, and I dare say a few Blues, would have you trapped for centuries in the Spire to eke out every scrap in your pretty little heads. Knowledge is power, and they hold knowledge above all else."

"Yes, Mother." They both answered.

"But," Luigh asked Maia, "what is the *Spire?*"

Maia looked Luigh dead-pan in the eyes for what felt like hours to Aislinn until Luigh sheepishly said, "….Mother."

Maia gave a snort of disgust at the disrespect of waiting so long for the title and said, "The Spire is the center of Occursum. It is where we Quia call home. Students also live and work there. It contains lecture halls, residences, and storage levels in the basement. You will be given a quick introduction of where you are allowed to go and where *not* to go."

"Mother?" Luigh pressed, "Who is in charge of all that?"

It was Maia's turn to now lecture her two young, by her standards, students.

"The Primus Princeps is the leader of the Quia. She is elected by a quorum from each Septem. She swears an oath on top of the Servire Et Tueri to uphold the laws and customs of Occursum. The Scriba Ad Primum is the Secretary to the Primus Princeps. She sees to the day-to-day operations of the Spire and is Keeper of the Keys."

Now, it was Aislinn's turn to be inquisitive, "What is Servire Et Tueri, Mother?"

Maia turned her head toward Aislinn and smiled as she answered her, "Servire Et Tueri is an oath all Quia take when they pass their final test and become true Quia. The oath is threefold: 1. Tell no lies, 2. Do no harm, except in self-defense or against Viventem, and 3. Make no weapon except against Viventem. The oath is taken on a Medi Obiectum, which binds the oath to the user in an unbreakable bond to the bones of the user. And, before you ask child, a Medi Obiectum is an object that has been infused or made with Medeis for a specific function. They are leftovers from a long-ago time, some from before the War of Power, some during, most we don't know the use for. The ones that we have found to be dangerous are locked away deep beneath the Spire. Others are carefully studied by a few of the Blue Septem. We classify these objects of power into three categories: Imo, Medi, and Alta. Imo Obiectum are the most numerous and tend to have the most benign results, such as glow like a candle and can be used by normal people. Medi Obiectum are more scarce and have been known to kill many Blues during experimentation. Alta Obiectum are the rarest of all; only a handful have been found."

"How do you differentiate between the types, Mother?" Aislinn asked.

Maia arched an eyebrow at Aislinn. "That is an excellent question for a Blue," Maia said to Aislinn, "But, I'd wait until you are at least a Third-Year before asking."

Maia winked at Aislinn, who sheepishly smiled back. Maia looked up toward the oppressive yellow burning giant ball of gas in the hazy sky and announced, "Let us find some shade and take our midday meal."

As if on cue, Angus came riding back at a slow trot and motioned to a mostly overgrown path off to his left and the group's right.

"I would have missed that." Farr remarked to Damara.

"Don't feel so bad, mo chridhe. I think I would have missed it as well if I was just travelling." She said to him.

The group followed Angus into the bush along the overgrown path to a grove of Willow trees that clung to their green summer leaves, surrounding an ever-shrinking pond. The group dismounted and tied their steads to one of the Willow trees. Aislinn and Luigh already went to the surrounding brush to gather wood and twigs; Farr and Damara also went in search of some game to eat. Maia gathered stones for the campfire. All in all, the group automatically went about the tasks they had grown accustomed to.

"BOY!" The shout from Angus almost startled even Maia.

Rowan lifted his head up just enough for Angus to see his eyes.

"Get off your horse and tend to them all, or you'll get another lesson about daydreaming." Angus gruffly commanded him.

Rowan gave a big audible sigh and slowly slid off his saddle. He took his horses' reigns and tied them on the Willow tree with the others. He made his way to the pack horse as if his feet were mired in thick wet clay. Obviously not happy nor enthusiastic with his routine chore.

Angus glared at Rowan for a few minutes to make sure he had set about caring for the horses, then he walked over to Maia.

"Something is troubling him."

"I know. I can sense it, but it's not the madness…not yet."

Maia watched Rowan laboriously carry a buck of water from the pond to the horses.

"Keep your eye on him. He may need you for what I'll do."

Angus looked at her, and only those that knew him would recognize the surprise on his stony face.

The girls returned with more than enough wood and kindling for a lunchtime fire, as the area had been dry for weeks. Maia had Luigh start the fire this time, and it took her three attempts, almost igniting her sleeve once.

"You're getting better at it." Aislinn commended her.

Luigh furrowed her sweat-beaded brow at Aislinn and grunted a thank you.

"Fire is a difficult element of Medeis for women to finesse. From now on, you will practice it, so you can test your *theories*." Maia told Luigh.

"Yes, Mother." Luigh acknowledged.

Farr and Damara returned with a few rabbits and a deer.

"We eat well, thanks to my Farr!" Damara beamed as she slapped his back. Farr stumbled a few steps with a giddy smile on his face while Aislinn and Luigh laughed at the Lacerten. They had already cleaned their bounty, and the four of them set to cooking all the meat.

Rowan finished tending to the horses and sat down against one of the willows.

"Rowan!" Farr called over to him. "Come over here!"

Rowan bowed his head down, hiding it under the hood, and sighed. *How can they be happy? We, more like me, are still being hunted by something with this power we know nothing of,* he thought, *there's no escape for me on this planet.*

"Rowan!" Farr yelled again.

Blowing air out of his mouth, Rowan got up and slowly made his way over to the campfire.

"Yeah?" He moaned at Farr.

"I'm starved, aren't you?" Farr asked as he motioned at the cooking meal.

"Eh." Rowan moaned.

"Eh?" Farr asked incredulously, knowing Rowan's normally voracious appetite.

"I guess." Rowan exasperatedly said.

Farr looked concernedly at Rowan but let the conversation drop.

It didn't take long for the food to cook, and the whole group began to eat.

"How much further to the next village?" Rowan asked Maia.

No response.

"Maia, I said, how much further to the next village??" Rowan repeated.

Again, Maia ignored him.

"Excuse me, Maia?" Farr asked"

Maia looked at Farr, "Yes?"

"How much further to the next village?" Farr said, repeating Rowan's question.

"If we maintain our current pace, I would say we should be there by dinner tomorrow," Maia answered Farr.

Rowan glared at Maia, then looked at Farr. Farr simply shrugged his shoulders. The rest of the group watched Rowan and Maia's exchange, or lack thereof. The air hung like a thunderstorm was off in the distance, and the group wondered if it would come their way or pass by without incident. The rest of the meal was decidedly quiet.

After the short meal conversation, the group packed up more solemnly than their arrival. Rowan grumbled under his hood, *What a bitch,* with an occasional shooting of daggered looks at Maia.

They made their way back to the road and continued their standard riding order to the next campsite on their way to the next village.

Rowan wondered, *Is she truly ignoring me on purpose? Hmm. Let's test it.*

Rowan rode his horse up the line to Maia's.

"….so, you see that everything that is or was alive is made up of cells." Luigh was telling Maia.

"Ah, I see," Maia replied.

"Um, excuse me, Maia?" Rowan asked, trying to mimic how Farr said it back at lunchtime.

"Please, child, continue," Maia instructed Luigh.

Luigh looked at Maia, then at Rowan, then back at Maia, then to Aislinn for help. Aislinn shrugged her shoulders, her eyebrows raised and brow furrowed; she was worried about what to do as well as Luigh.

"Um, sorry, Mother, but I think Rowan had asked a question?" Luigh tried to say meekly and diplomatically.

"I know. Please continue your Biology 101 lesson, child," Maia matter-of-factly said to Luigh.

Luigh looked at Rowan, scrunching her nose and shrugging her shoulders, when Maia sharply said, "Now, child."

Luigh jumped up straight in her saddle.

"Yes, mother." Luigh sullenly said.

Rowan stiffened up in his saddle and was about to unleash a tirade on Maia. His left hand was gripping the hilt of his sword so tight his knuckles were turning white. He was starting to lift his right hand with a pointed finger at Maia when a deep gravelly voice like an avalanche of slate rocks cascading down a mountainside came from his blind side.

"Boy, come with me and learn how to scout," Angus said to Rowan.

The sound of that avalanche startled Rowan out of his burning frustration at Maia.

Rowan turned to his left to Angus and said, "Wha? Oh. Yeah, I guess so."

"Try to curb your enthusiasm, boy." Angus mocked.

Rowan gave a slight chuckle at Angus' sarcasm. He knew he was being sullen the past few days. *Perhaps scouting will give me the chance to slip away and keep them safe.* Rowan shot Maia, Luigh, and Aislinn a last look over his shoulder, making Aislinn shiver before he spurred his horse forward with Angus. *They have* her *now to protect them*, he contemptuously thought.

Aislinn watched Rowan ride ahead with Angus, her forehead and face wrinkled. *Why does he look so sad?*

"…right, Ais?" Luigh asked a distracted Aislinn.

"Child!" Maia quipped.

Aislinn shook her head, "Huh?"

"Pay attention, child," Maia sternly said to Aislinn, "*He* has his instruction, as do you. Best you keep your concentration where it belongs."

"Yes, Mother," Aislinn said like a scolded child caught with a stolen cookie.

On the opposite side of the group, Farr and Damara looked at each other. Neither knew what to make of the last few hours of the changed group dynamic.

This pall over the group continued even as they stopped for a late dinner. The sun was setting over the Western Mountains, and the air was finally cooling off. Everyone went about their usual 'making camp' chores; Rowan was still mopey but didn't need to be spurred to take care of the horses. But, the group dynamic was evident in how they were arranged during dinner. Maia, Aislinn, and Luigh all sat next to each other. Farr and Damara sitting next to each other but across the fire from them. Angus and Rowan ate their meal off aways near the horses, then slipped away into the surrounding forest, and didn't reappear until the others in the group were fast asleep.

Farr awoke the next morning with Damara snuggled up against his backside.

Morning love," he said as he turned his head to face her. She gently put her hand on the side of his head, leaned in, and intimately caressed his lips with hers.

After enjoying the embrace for a few moments, Farr pulled back and turned his whole body toward Damara.

"Perhaps, "he started, "I can speak to Rowan today and discover what is troubling him."

"From what I see, love," she said to him, "I wouldn't press it. It is best not to get in the middle of a Quia situation."

"But, Rowan is not Quia," Farr said.

"Yes, but Maia is," Damara pointed out, "and Angus is her Gleidhidh. There is a plan there, even if it is not obvious."

"I will heed your advice for now, love, and tread lightly," Farr replied as he softly traced the outline of her cheek, "but Rowan is my friend, and I will protect him."

Farr sat up and stretched his arms out. *This whole experience of sleeping under the stars is almost like my youth back home,* he mused, *well, almost.* He looked around the campsite for Rowan, but he and Angus had already gone into the woods, no doubt on a scouting lesson. Instead, he saw Maia, Aislinn, and Luigh sitting by the campfire, engrossed in a lesson or lecture of some sort.

"Shall we prepare ourselves for another small hunt?" Farr asked Damara.

"I believe we have enough cooked meat till midday, mo chridhe. Lay with me a while longer." She crooned at him.

With a sly smile, Farr winked at her, "As you wish."

The group tarried for a while when Maia stood up and announced it was time to get moving. Luigh and Aislinn began to do their camp-breaking chores, and Farr and Damara helped them. Rowan and Angus appeared from the forest underbrush at an angle that even surprised Damara.

"He learns quickly." She said, looking down at Farr. He grunted in affirmation up at her while looking at Rowan with narrowed, studying, tilted jewelel-like eyes.

The group packed up and rode out to the road. This time, the group lineup was very different than what it had been. Rowan went off with Angus in the lead; Maia, Aislinn, and Luigh rode close together, lost in conversation; and Farr and Damara rode several paces in the rear next to each other.

This new group dynamic continued throughout the hot, hazy oppressive day, even through the midday meal. They didn't camp for lunch; Maia wanted to make up time for the late morning start. Farr and Damara didn't know they were coming up on the village. It had been so warm that very few fires were burning. Instead, Rowan and Angus' sudden return drew their attention. They rounded a slight bend to the right, and Maia announced, "Welcome to West Fork Town."

Chapter 11

M aia motioned for Farr and Damara to ride closer as Rowan and Angus joined them.

"As before, let Angus and I do all the speaking. If asked, I am Mary, and Angus is Andrew."

Rowan, Aislinn, Luigh, Damara, and Farr nodded in agreement. Maia took that as a signal and rode out to lead the group, with Angus and Rowan close behind. Aislinn, Luigh, Farr, and Damara rode clumped together a horse length after Angus and Rowan.

Maia led them down what Rowan thought was Main Street until he saw a street sign that read "North Mountain Road". The road was well packed down, with dust clouds kicked up from horses, carts, and people. Many people were crossing here and there across the street to visit the various shops lining each side of the broad road. Rowan glanced back at Farr and saw the Lacerten was studying the road and construction of the town. West Fork Town was similar in its building construction to the far northern village they had first encountered upon descending from the mountains. Cobblestone first levels with maple, oak, and chestnut upper levels, with wood shingles for roofs. The stark difference in this town versus the small mountain village was the buildings reached four or five stories. This town also seemed to buzz with more activity that seemed almost out of place to Rowan, but he couldn't put his finger on it. He watched in awe and checked a few times to see if his mouth was open; as the townsfolk greeted each other as they were about their day, occasional laughter would rise up from a meeting or two.

The group rode past another wide road that led off to the East; the street sign marking it as "Das Daingneach Road" and the road they were still upon was labeled "Mächtige Mauer Road". Maia led them down the first side street to their right and then right again down an alleyway wide enough for two horse carts to pass each other. The alleyway, flanked by two tall buildings, opened up to a small road that led behind the buildings on Mächtige Mauer Road and left down the side street buildings. The group followed Maia to the left alleyway, and she stopped at a four-story building with a stable on the right. Two stable boys came out to greet them. Maia spoke with them, but Rowan was too busy looking at the back of the building, trying to figure out what the sign near the back door meant, to hear what was said.

"Boy!" Angus cracked at Rowan.

A little startled by Angus, Rowan shot up a little in his saddle and quickly looked around, his right hand instinctively grabbing the hilt of his sword and barred an inch of its steel. He felt the rush of blood to the capillaries in his cheeks, and the tip of his nose itched a little as his embarrassment became obvious. He saw that the rest of the group had dismounted. The horses were already being led into the stable, and he was still sitting upon his horse.

Rowan sheathed his sword and shrugged, eking out a mumbled "sorry."

He dismounted and one of the stable boys, who was hesitantly waiting, rushed out to take Rowan's horse. Angus glared at Rowan, Aislinn and Luigh shook their heads at him, Damara had a puzzled look like she just discovered him, and Farr, with a furrowed brow, looked concerned. Maia, completely ignoring Rowan, was already walking to the now apparent Inn's backdoor.

"Everything alright?" Farr asked Rowan.

"Oh yeah," Rowan shook his head and held his hand up to his diminutive friend, "I was just trying to read the sign."

"Ahh," Farr unfurred his brow and smiled, "that would be a good question for Aislinn. I do not recognize it either." Farr took up Damara's left hand and looked up at her, "Shall we?"

Damara clasped her hand in his, intertwining her long fingers with his, and smiled at him. The pair walked toward the Inn's back door, leaving Rowan in the alleyway looking at the printed sign "Gasthaus mit lila Heidekraut".

A minute or two passed, then Rowan was on the ground, face down in the hard dirt, dust stinging his eyes, nose, mouth, and lungs when he suddenly sucked in the air after having it forcibly pushed out from the impact. He pushed off his hands, pulling his feet up underneath his hips, and sprang up and to his left, drawing his sword. He blinked as fast as he could and rubbed his stinging watery eyes to try and get the dust out, as his lungs hacked wildly to do the same.

"At least you didn't stay down." Came the gravely sound from the tall wide blurry man in front of Rowan. "Now get your arse inside, whelp."

Rowan recognized Angus' voice and relaxed, putting the sword tip on the ground and leaning the hilt on his waist. He rubbed at both his eyes and finally cleaned them enough to see an irate mountain in front of him. He gave a good final cough to clear the particles from his lungs and sheathed his sword.

"Gee," Rowan began to quip, "Thanks for checking on me."

"Get. Your. Arse. Inside. Whelp." Angus said, his eyes burning a cold blue intensity at each period and articulate intonation.

Rowan sighed and went into the back of the Inn, quick-stepping past Angus like a child afraid of a spanking. *If nothing else, I would be free of Mr. Mountain and his handler*, he chuckled to himself.

Rowan walked down the hallway from the back door, noticing a set of back stairs to his right, past a few entries on his left; the last one had two doors that swung out or in and sprang back to a closed position. *That must be the kitchen,* he correctly guessed. The kitchen butted up to a bar area and opened to a great room with three rows of six tables with a large fireplace on each side and a large door that spit the far wall with windows: the common room. *Don't these people have any different architectural designs??* Rowan questioned in his head.

With Angus close behind, Rowan made his way over to the table the rest of the group was already sitting at. *Oh! What a surprise! The corner table away from everyone!* Rowan thought sarcastically.

"Glad you could join us." Luigh admonished Rowan.

"I was trying to figure out what the sign at the back of the Inn said." Rowan sassily said back.

"Purple Heather Inn," Aislinn announced with pride and a smile.

"Impressive," Maia said to Aislinn, which made Aislinn blush.

"How do you know that?" Rowan said incredulously.

"I believe it's Germanic." Aislinn beamed.

"Oh great, another language to learn." Rowan scoffed.

"I know! Right?!" Aislinn all but squealed, lightly clapping her hands.

"Perhaps," Maia started to announce to the group as she quickly glanced at Angus, "Aislinn and I can give some brief introductory lessons while we rest here for a day or two to replenish supplies. We do need to make a choice as to whether we go East or South." Her gaze lingered on Rowan when she came to the end of her announcement.

Rowan more than felt her gaze, and he slunk down on the bench to make himself smaller. *Does she really expect me to decide??* He worried; *I am not from here. She has ignored me for the past two days, and now she expects ME to make the decision for the whole group? I don't belong here. I've got to get away!*

Maia watched Rowan attempt to shrink from her sight and turned her attention back to the rest of the group, "For now, eat, and rest tonight. We can discuss this further tomorrow."

Maia had apparently booked three rooms, unlike the usual operating procedure of two rooms split by gender. Rowan was initially confused by this but then felt like an imbecile when he realized *girl room, boy room, and couple's room.* Farr and Damara had a room across from Angus and Rowan, while Maia, Aislinn, and Luigh had the room next to the boys.

Rowan shook his head, smiled, and gave Farr a small salute as he watched them go into their room. *Glad they will finally get some 'alone' time. Good for them!* Rowan happily thought for Farr. He turned around and saw Angus waiting by their room, door open. The warden waiting for the prisoner to go to his cell. Rowan's happiness for his friend evaporated like a drop of water in the desert as he begrudgingly shuffled his feet while he slowly walked into his room.

Angus followed Rowan into the room and closed the door with a thud that shook Rowan and made him a little nervous for the lecture he felt was coming.

None came.

Angus simply went to the bed near the door and laid down upon it.

Rowan's felt his eyes widen in sudden wonderment. *No lecture about me being a petulant child??* He thought, *huh.* Rowan walked around to the second bed, looking at the room. It was slightly larger than the last room he stayed in, similar to the Unicorn but not as nice as the Keep. The furniture was a sturdy wood, maple, or oak; he couldn't tell. Two small four-drawer dressers separated by a side table against one wall, two full-sized wooden beds with a small wood-burning stove between them, and a small bed table on the other side of them. Two high-backed chairs and a small round coffee table by the window.

Rowan walked over to the window, testing the plushness of one of the chair backs as he looked out. *Eh, not as comfy feeling as the Keep's chairs*, he reminisced. Rowan could see the building right next door outside the second-story window. There was about a three-foot gap between them. The building next door had a ledge beneath the second-story windows that ran across it that looked like it went all the way around the building. *Hmm*, Rowan thought.

"Get some sleep." Angus quietly commanded, removing Rowan from his thoughts.

"Fine." Rowan acquiesced.

Rowan looked once more at the ledge, and his room's window, then went to his bed.

He waited for what felt like hours, pretending to sleep by taking deep, restful breaths. It almost did make him fall asleep, as it was almost soothing. Finally, he felt like Mr. Mountain was truly asleep enough to make his move, and Rowan opened his eyes to the now darkened room.

Rowan waited for his eyes to adjust to the dim light coming from under the door and tested Angus' slumber by slowly sitting up.

Nothing from Angus.

Rowan slowly swung his legs over the side of the bed that faced the window.

Not a stir from the other bed.

Rowan slowly stood up.

Angus sucked in a deep breath.

Rowan held his.

Angus let out a snort and resumed his sleep.

Rowan slowly let his breath out and slowly tiptoed toward the side table, stopping at each step to look over his shoulder toward the black mass that was Angus.

No movement.

Rowan gingerly picked up his pack and made it to the window. *Now to open it.*

Rowan removed the leather gloves from his hands for better grip and tucked them in his belt behind his back. He then slowly worked his fingers under the lower windowpane.

Nothing from the black mass.

He slowly worked the window back and forth as he pulled it up. The wood gave tiny squeaks as they rubbed against each other. Rowan's heart stopped with each squeak, and he held his breath, expecting Angus to spring up and come at him.

Nothing.

The window was now up and open. *Almost there!* Rowan thought, *now the hard part of fitting through!!*

Rowan unbuckled his sword and rolled the belt around it, being careful not to let it clink. Holding it in his left hand, he carefully put his right leg out of the window and stretched it toward the ledge. His foot reached most of it, with his heel hanging off. He ducked his head under and out of the window, looking back one last time at Angus.

The black mass on the bed didn't move.

He pushed off with his right hand on the windowsill, left foot in the room, and somewhat leaped for the ledge.

His chest hit the wooden wall with a thwack, and he almost dropped his sword. *That's gonna sting for a bit*, Rowan thought, resisting the urge to rub his chest. Inching his way along the ledge on the balls and toes of his feet, he made it to the back of the building and alleyway. The building had a small wooden awning over its backdoor, presumably for deliveries. Rowan tested his weight on the edge of the awning, and it held. He mostly slid down it and landed in the alleyway on his feet with a very audible thud. Rowan quickly ducked under the awning, holding the sword to his chest, and held his breath. He waited for half a minute and peeked up and out from the awning.

Nothing.

Rowan made his way down the alley to the first opening and side street, buckling his sword back on and pulling on the black leather gloves. *I'll backtrack back up and into the mountains. That was remote enough and far enough from everything that they would all be safe. Away from me.*

Farr and Damara were awoken by a pounding on their door. Farr rubbed his eyes and stretched.

"Downstairs, and fast little man!" Angus commanded through the closed oak door.

"Uh oh," Farr quietly said to Damara as he gently rolled onto her chest, "What did Rowan do now?"

Damara cocked an eyebrow, "It is not wise to anger a Gleidhidh."

"We best hurry," Farr said, giving her a quick peck and a wink, rolling off of her, and dropping himself down onto the floor.

The pair got dressed as fast as possible and made their way down to the common room with alacrity.

Farr stopped suddenly halfway across the floor; his superior hearing kicked in.

"…gone?!? What do you mean GONE!" Luigh demanded while she reached up and repeatedly poked Angus in the chest.

Farr grabbed Damara's hand and soberly quick walked to the table.

"It appears he slipped out of the window in the middle of the night." Angus calmly said to Luigh, totally and intentionally ignoring her pokes.

"We have to go after him!" Aislinn emphatically insisted.

"Sit." Maia soothingly said to everyone.

Luigh, Aislinn, Farr, and Damara slowly sat opposite Maia. Angus remained standing. Maia looked up at him, and he grunted before sitting next to her.

"He can't have gotten far in a few hours and most likely will need rest. We can catch up to wherever he has gone." Maia calmly said.

"But which direction?" Farr asked.

"His tracks went back North," Angus replied. "I followed it for a few blocks before returning and alerting you all."

"Well then, let's get going!" Luigh demanded.

"First, we eat. He is on foot, and we have horses. We will catch up quickly. Do not worry, child." Maia said, trying to calm Luigh.

"Ugh!" Luigh said as she let her palms hit the table with a thud. "Yes, Mother," she said begrudgingly.

The group was almost done with breakfast when the front door to the Inn opened wide. Three prominent men, obscured by the sunlight streaming in behind them, stormed in.

"A chù! Dè tha a' dèanamh an seo?" came a familiar voice to the group.

Chapter 12

A ngus sprang to his feet so fast Maia and the bench they occupied almost went backward. Farr, Aislinn, Luigh, and Damara squinted against the bright incoming beam of morning sunlight to see the newcomer through his shadow. Farr and Aislinn both knew the voice of that particular shadow well, especially Farr. He didn't think he would ever see that gruff man again, remembering the many grumblings, the many lessons, and the almost touching goodbye – well as touching as Farr thought a grizzled old warrior from Parva Frater could be.

Damara watched Farr as he slowly stood up. Angus had already closed the distance to the front door and clasped hands with the shadow man. The pair walked back to the group's table.

No one had noticed Maia was standing until they all had watched Angus and the shadow man approach her side of the table.

"Hail and well met," Maia said to the shadow man, "Master Glenn."

"Thank you, and you as well," he winked back. Then he turned his attention to Farr and Aislinn. "I see my little prince and princess have acquitted themselves."

"Indeed, they have, Master Glenn," Maia said with a proud motherly smile, "all in thanks to your tutelage, I'm sure."

"We can regal you of our travels later, Naill," Angus gruffly interrupted, "but what brings you so far from the Keep?"

Master Glenn leaned up close to Angus, making his 5' 8" height somehow almost equal to Angus', and he whispered with a growl and a smile, "War!"

Maia's eyes widened, and she hurriedly said, "I'm sure you would like to freshen up, Master Glenn. Please let me offer our rooms."

"Ah, um, yes. Thank you, Mistress." Naill said as he looked around the common room.

Maia gave an ever-slight nod, "Follow me, please." She glided from the table and up the stairs with Angus and Naill in tow like a mother duck and her ducklings.

Aislinn and Farr were still somewhat dumbstruck from Naill's sudden appearance, Damara took the whole scene in as a common occurrence, but Luigh had a perplexed look on her face.

She looked from Aislinn to Farr back to Aislinn and scowled. "Who the hell is that?!" she finally demanded.

Damara, the only calm one left at the table, stood up, gently nudged Farr, and said, "Perhaps we follow and find out?"

Far shook himself out of his daze, and he and Damara made for the main stairs that led to their rooms. Luigh stood up in a huff and pulled Aislinn's sleeve. "Let's go."

Luigh and Aislinn caught up with Farr and Damara in the hallway leading to their rooms. They guessed that Maia would use her room and made for that door. They listened for a brief second and heard nothing.

"Can you see it?" Aislinn asked Luigh.

"No, what??"

"There's a thin web of air bubbling out from the room."

"A trap?"

"No, I don't think so. It reminds me of the domes she made at previous camps."

Luigh gave a satisfied nod, flattened out the front of her dress, drew herself up to her 5 feet of height, and stormed into the room without knocking.

"Ah, children," Maia announced.

She was sitting in one of the modestly plush highbacked chairs by the window. Angus off to one side behind her and Naill Glenn in front of her. *A Queen holding court*, Luigh scoffed in her head as she marched right up to the only other vacant chair in the room, next to Maia. She glared at Maia as she crossed the room, then sat down without giving her a second glance.

"And whom do we have here?" Luigh asked Naill.

Naill raised his left eyebrow causing his large scar that ran to his jaw to stretch.

"You remember Master of Arms Naill Glenn from Das Daingneach, child?" Maia calmly said to Luigh.

"Ah, yes. Good to see you again, Master Glenn." Luigh said, looking straight into Naill's blue eyes.

"Please, continue, Master Glenn," Maia said as cool as a summer stream.

"Ah, yes, Maia Quia, well, ahem," Naill started as he cleared his gravelly throat, "King Caisteal received word that two months ago, an army from Meridiem crossed into Ventus. Normally, we wouldn't get involved in such a lowland border thing, but they have a man with them. A man that can do things."

"What *things*?" Maia said, sitting forward in her chair. Farr could hear Angus' armor creak under the strain of muscles tightening.

"It has been reported that he wields Medeis," Naill said, "as a weapon. They lay waste and burn everything in their path."

Maia sat back in her chair and smoothed out her lap. "And Occursum?" she asked.

"They have dispatched a conclave almost the same time we set out," Naill reported.

Maia let out a thoughtful sigh as she sat back in the chair. "Our plans change yet again."

There was palpable tension as the entirety of the room waited in silence for Maia to illuminate them to her thoughts.

"Master Glenn, when does your host leave?" Maia asked.

"On the morrow, Maia Quia."

"Good. I and the children will accompany you. Please inform Lieutenant MacGill."

"As you command, Maia Quia." Naill said as he pressed his fist to his chest in salute and strode out of the room.

"Wait. What?!" Luigh exploded on Maia as she shot up to her feet, hands on her hips, "You are sooo not going to lead *us* into a war!"

"Hush child," Maia calmly said, "you do not know the plan yet."

Farr heard Angus' armor creak even more under the strain of his muscles, like a volcano about to erupt. From what Farr could guess, Angus did not like the plan.

Maia stood up and faced Luigh. "Luigh, please take Aislinn, Farr, and Damara to the next room. I would like a private word with Angus." Maia coolly said as she took Luigh's hand in hers.

Luigh's shoulders dropped, releasing the tension she held in her confrontation.

"Yes. Mother," she said sullenly. She turned to the others and jerked her head toward the door, "Let's go."

Aislinn's jaw was on the floor, and Farr's eyes couldn't get any wider. *Did that just happen?!?!* Aislinn thought incredulously. *Luigh didn't even put up a fight!*

"Come!" Luigh snapped at Aislinn.

Aislinn jumped and pulled on Farr's arm as the four left Maia's room next door.

Once Maia saw the door was shut behind the four, she turned to Angus.

"Find Rowan. He needs you now more than ever. I know you do not like this, but you will know where I am and how to find me. I will be fine. They sent a conclave. I need to find one of my Septem's shops. Regina must be informed."

Angus tensed up, his armor threatening to pop off him in an explosion, "As you wish, Maia Quia."

Maia entered what was Rowan and Angus' room and looked around. She saw Aislinn and Damara sitting on the ends of the beds, Farr in a high-backed chair, and Luigh in the other. She stood there a moment and took them all in.

"Children," she began, "I have no intention of breaking my oath to you and intentionally putting you in harm's way."

Luigh gave a satisfied grunt and quick nod of her head. Maia shot her a look.

"However," Maia continued, "You have been in danger ever since you arrived. I have started some of you on a long journey on how to defend yourselves and others," she looked at Aislinn and Luigh. "Some of you took the initiative and learned a useful skill and have become highly proficient," she looked at Farr, "and some of you already know how to take care of yourself." She looked at Damara. "We will travel with Master Glenn for protection, as well as some companionship. We have lost most of our supplies. If nothing else, we can travel with them until we reach the crossroads to Occursum in Ventus. Master Glenn informs me that a

Conclave was dispatched. 12 Quia is worth 12,000 armored men on horseback. There will be nothing to fear from this threat from Meridiem."

"Mother?" Aislinn asked, "What about Rowan??"

"Do not worry, child," Maia said soothingly, "Angus will find him, and then they will find us."

"Beg your pardon, but I want to go help find Rowan." Farr interrupted.

Aislinn and Luigh were surprised by the Lacertan's brashness. Damara smiled at her love's loyalty.

"A boon you would be to aid Angus," Maia said, "but I fear the group needs both you," she looked from Farr to Damara, "and Damara more in a scouting role. Master Glenn speaks highly of you."

Farr blushed at the compliment.

"Besides, I feel that Rowan needs Angus more than us at the moment."

Luigh let out an audible scoff that drew Maia's stern gaze.

"Issue, child?" Maia asked.

That was all the opening Luigh was waiting for.

"I get travelling with Master Glenn for protection. The supply issue could be solved here in this *town*, and what makes you an authority on Rowan? You don't know him. You didn't raise him. You've gone out of your way to ignore him. Hell! You aren't from the same *planet*!"

Maia inhaled a deep breath, centered herself, and let it out.

"Child," she serenely said, "True, I did not know Rowan, nor come from the same place, *but* I know what he is *now*. Do you?"

"If you know he has changed the way we have, then why aren't you helping him like us? Nooooo, you'd rather ignore him and force him in the opposite direction!"

"Enough, child. I will not explain every child-rearing method to you. You swore an oath to me. I am keeping mine to you. I expect the same."

Luigh sunk back into the chair. Ideas, thoughts, and unasked questions swirling in her head.

"Yes…mother." Luigh sullenly said with a hint of sarcasm.

Maia arched her eyebrow. "Stay here until I return. I have a quick errand to run." Maia didn't wait for the obligatory 'yes, Mother' answer, quickly turning on her toes, causing her dress to puff out, and left the room.

As soon as the door closed, Luigh sat forward and exclaimed, "I knew it!"

Everyone's confused eyes turned toward her.

"Knew what?" Aislinn asked.

Luigh looked at her and quietly whispered, "He has Medeis, and that scares *Mother Maia.*"

"Whoa," Aislinn said as she gripped the bed frame as if the world had just shaken. Farr looked concerned for his friend, but Damara; Damara was genuinely scared and nervous.

Chapter 13

Maia closed the door to the room, leaving Luigh, Aislinn, Farr, and Damara inside. *Still petulant, but a little more pliable*, she thought, *I have to be sure not to totally break that stubbornness. She will need every bit of it for what is to come.* Maia strode down the hallway, down the main steps into the common room, and out the Inn's front doors. She turned left toward Mächtige Mauer Road and continued until it became Das Daingneach Road. She continued a few blocks more. The streets were beginning to pick up the everyday hustle and bustle of the morning. Hawkers shouting their wares from streetside carts, moderately dressed women in stout wools window shopping at various shops. Farm-dressed men and young boys in wools that have been well used and repaired with multiple patches riding in carts carrying supplies from outlying farms and ranches. All before the blistering sun cleared the tops of the smaller second-story buildings.

Maia looked both ways and quickly crossed the road, dodging between the back of one empty cart heading out of the town and a horse's nose of a cart full of hay coming into the town. The dust from the wagons and morning traffic was just beginning to permeate the air and clung to anything below the shin. *I fear I will have to do another wash when I get back*, Maia annoyedly thought about the ambient conditions. She made her way north to the next block and turned right, striding down the side street.

The road wasn't particularly long, as it angled north to connect to another side street. It had a few smaller specialty shops on either side; a seamstress, barber, thatcher, carpenter, a small Inn, and a herbologist. It was the last she sought out.

The front window of the tiny shop was typical and nondescript, with groups of drying herbs tied together and hung by their stems arranged by type and use, small potted green herbs in the windowsill. By all accounts, it was a very typical herbologist's shop. But to a Quia, there was, etched in the top right corner of the shop's doorframe, a small triangle that indicated it was far from an ordinary shop.

Maia entered the shop, and a small bell rang as the door opened and closed. An elderly woman came out of a back room and stood behind a counter.

"Yes? May I help you, dear?"

Feeling a sense of urgency, Maia didn't have time for the usual pleasantries of passwords and catchphrases. Instead, she walked up to the counter, took hold of Medeis, and used thin threads of Air to make a gold Occursum coin float out from her belt purse to the countertop.

"Oh. I see." The old shopkeeper said as her eyes widened with acknowledgement.

"I need access to your roof, please," Maia asked her.

"Through the back and to the right, Mother." The geriatric lady said with a smile.

"Thank you, daughter," Maia replied.

Maia made her way through the back room containing labeled barrels of dried herbs, some sealed and some open and in various states of capacity. The ceiling rafters had multiple spaced-out nails with more drying herbs, a small desk and workstation with empty terracotta pots, and pots filled with dark rich soil waiting to be seeded. The musky, sweet aroma from so many herbs was almost overpowering in the back room and caused Maia to wrinkle and itch her nose as she made her way to the stairs.

Maia climbed her way up the steep narrow stairs to the third floor. The top floor wasn't much of a floor per se, but a single small room with just enough space for a writing desk with many cubbies above it. If Maia or any other Quia were known to be in this town, there would be a message waiting for her in one of these cubbies; they were all empty. *At least no one knows I'm here, and there are no other Sisters.* She took up the quill and a small slip of paper, penning a quick short sentence. After drying the ink with a small sprinkling of sand, she carefully rolled the note tightly. Maia placed it into a small cylinder, sealed it with wax, and pressed it with a small ring from her belt pouch. She exited the door to the flat roof on the other side of the room. Maia was greeted with the many cooing sounds of pigeons of various coloring from black, grey, mottled, and white. Each bird had its own modest cage to not release the others when one was selected. Maia chose a mottled avian, opened the cage with one hand, and quickly but gently grasped the bird's breast and wings. She tucked her sealed cylinder into another on the pigeon's leg and released it. Maia watched as the bird circled a few times, gaining altitude, then flew off in an easterly direction. As the bird was reduced to a small dot on the morning sky, Maia thought, *I hope that is*

enough, and started to make her way back to the
Inn and the others.

****

It had been over six months since Regina had any word from Maia. The last known location was in Baile Atha Cliath. Only rumors of an entire village northeast of which had been completely burned down, the ground turned to glass. She dispatched two trusted Quia to investigate and cover the area with dirt. They reported no feeling of Medeis used, no survivors, and no evidence of anything save a big circle of glass where a small village once stood.

Regina was taking her midday meal in her office on the third-highest floor of the Spire, the second highest would be her living quarters, and the top floor is the Roost where the carrier pigeons were kept. It was a Second Year's responsibility to care for, monitor, retrieve the sealed messages, and bring them to the Scriba Ad Primum, Genelia Quia. Regina had piles of papers and parchments in various sizes surrounding her plate of half-eaten chicken and mixed vegetables of green and orange. Regina would pick up a report and place it back in a pile, then pick up another from a different stack, only to replace it. She did this shuffling of papers throughout her lunch.

"Ahem, excuse me, Mother," came a hushed voice from the other side of Regina's desk.

Regina, holding yet another report, looked up. She had not noticed the olive-brown woman in a brilliant canary yellow dress with lace trimming in front of her. Regina was used to intrusions in her office, mainly by the same woman, so she was not very startled by the sudden speech. *But*, she thought as she put the report down on her desk, *how does she sneak in here without a sound?*

"Yes, Genelia?" Regina asked.

"Mother," Genelia took her job very seriously and always upheld the titles and traditions of the office, "a message for you." Genelia held out the tiny, sealed cylinder that contained a note. "I believe it is from a lost sheep."

Regina nodded and took the cylinder, broke the seal, unraveled the note, and read it to herself.

"Do we know where the bird came from?" Regina asked.

"Yes, Mother. From West Fork Town in Parva Frater." Genelia replied.

Regina collapsed back in her high-backed chair, made of maple and stained a dark chocolate, the edges carved with various horses. "I guessed correctly." She said her thought aloud.

"Mother?" Genelia inquired of the thought.

Regina blinked at the question, momentarily forgetting Genelia was in the room. She sat up in her chair in a regal manner and looked at Genelia with a twinkle in her eye that she would get when her plans went her way.

"The trouble in Ventus *is* a False Phoenix," Regina explained as she handed the tiny note to Genelia.

Genelia took the note with a puzzled look on her face and uncurled it.

> *Nest found in the North. Crows gave chase. Two hatchlings bound for home; another rooster kept safe.*

Genelia slowly handed back the note to Regina. "It seems you have, Mother." She said with a sly smile.

"Anything else?" Regina asked.

"Nothing as important, just a few more reports of rats trying to get into the lower levels."

"I suppose we need more *cats.*"

"As you wish, Mother."

Genelia gave a slight bow and left the room without making a sound.

I seriously need to find out where she gets her slippers made, Regina thought as she carefully put the note in a small letterbox, she kept on her desk. She locked the box, used Medeis to place a ward on it to stop any prying eyes, and picked up another report from yet another pile on her desk.

A Conclave, fifty Gleidhidh, plus another thousand troops from King Caisteal should be more than enough, she thought as she read the letter from King Caisteal. *But where are Bella and Kiona? I should have heard by now that they caught Gildred. The last note from them was south of Mächtige Mauer a month ago. Yes, I sent enough*, she thought, reassuring herself as she replaced the letter from King Caisteal and picked up another.

Chapter 14

R owan snuck along the dark alleyway and made his way to the front of the Inn. *The fastest way out of this town is the way I came in,* he thought, *I have to keep them safe.* He took one last look up at the second story of the Inn and walked quickly up the side street to Mächtige Mauer Road and continued until it became Das Daingneach Road. He hurriedly made his way out of the sleeping town and began to jog northward a few miles before making his own trail to the west. Rowan used what Angus had taught him to cover his tracks into the wild forest for almost a mile off the road. This wilderness deception trick he learned from Angus along with his limited training in flight school slowed him down, and he ran as fast as he dared amongst the roots, dips, rocks, and sudden rises in the forest.

Rowan ran out of steam a few miles deeper into the woods, the terrain becoming more cumbersome and beginning to rise in elevation. It had been a few hours since he slipped out of West Fork Town, and he guessed that the sun would start to rise in a couple more by the increase in light and a dark violet glow off to the East. He walked a few more miles, backtracking to cross a small river and a large outcropping of granite. Rowan's stomach reminded him that it was almost time for breakfast, and his brain was getting foggy. He settled on a small flat rock that split a wide shallow stream. He rummaged in his backpack and dug out some rolls he had saved from last night's dinner. *Ugh, I did not think this out too clearly. I wish I had Farr's bow!*

After eating a couple of the rolls, he put one back into his pack and looked through it to inventory his food in the growing ambient light. *Two rolls, three carrots, some sort of baked potato, and a handful of green beans. Ugh, one, maybe two more meals at best. Maybe I can make a bow and some arrows? I do have some string, and I can make some squirrel snares. From their ribs, I might be able to make a fishing hook. Mmmm, what I would give for a nice big fish with some lemon.*

Rowan shook himself from his dining daydream, refilled his waterskin from the stream, and set off.

The forest of deciduous trees was thick, with dense underbrush, and Rowan remembered the tiny annoying biting midges. He pulled his hood up over his head as the heat of the day began to rise and activate the flying bloodsuckers. Rowan did his best to observe the teachings of Angus to not make a path or a visible trail as he made his way up toward the mountains they had initially come down.

Walking many miles and most of the morning, Rowan decided to stop and rest for a while. It had gotten too hot for even the flying insects. In fact, the only living thing that Rowan could discern to be awake in the heat of midday were cicadas, and they buzzed loudly and nonstop. He found a nice, secluded spot under a rock overhang near a small lake. The lake, scummed over with bright green algae, showed apparent signs of shrinkage from the evaporative heat. *I'm not going to chance refilling my waterskin in that*, Rowan thought as he turned his attention to the overhang. The rock was covered in a blue-green lichen, and there was a small maple tree attempting to grow on top of it. Rowan did his best to clear out what would be his roof from hanging roots, spiders, and other creepy-crawly insects with more legs than he could count. The ones with giant black pinchers gave him the willies. *Too bad I can't make a fire yet and burn these things*, he mused. Satisfied that the insects and arachnids were evicted, Rowan took off his cloak and laid it on the ground beneath the overhang. He laid down upon it and pulled up one side as he rolled onto his side to face the lake. Sleep overtook him immediately.

Rowan awoke with a start and slapped something off of his face. Imagining one of those things with the pincers trying to crawl into his ear and eat his brain, Rowan sprang up and began to flail his arms about himself, attempting to brush every inch off his body at once. He finally calmed down and looked at where his cloak was lying and about the ground. There he saw a colossal daddy-long-legs spider making its way from the hood of his cloak to the side of the overhang. Rowan gave a sigh of relief, picked his cloak up, and shook it out. A few sticks and dirt were all that fell off the cloak. *Luckily, no hitchhikers.* He looked out over the lake at the sky to try and judge the time of day. *Well into the afternoon. I best get moving.*

Rowan was about to put his cloak on when his stomach loudly announced it wanted attention. He opened up his pack and ate the carrots and green beans with the last two rolls. *Ugh, just the potato left. I better keep my eye open for a good stick or branch to make a bow.*

He closed the pack, settled it on his back, took his bearing off the sun, and decided on a northwestern path around the diminutive shrinking lake.

The way through the woods and up the foothills of the mountains became more arduous as Rowan walked. His speed had slowed, but he thought he was still making good time as the deciduous trees were giving way to more conifers. The underbrush was thinning out, and the ground was covered in more shale than granite rocks here and there. Rowan estimated that it must be about six in the evening, judging by the rumbling of his stomach and the fading light of the sun to the West. *Time to look for a place to settle down for the night.*

Rowan slowed his pace to a slow walk as he looked all around for a suitable place to make camp. There was a grove of cedar pines a few hundred yards ahead of him. *That should keep the creepy crawlies away.*

He made it to the cedar grove without an issue and gathered the fallen needles for bedding. He had found some flint amongst some shale a few miles back, along with some dry moss, and even though he wasn't going to or needed to have a fire, he decided to test out making a fire. Rowan took out a small flat piece of shale the size of a dinner plate from his bag and placed it on the ground; put a small handful of dried moss on the shale plate; took out another knife-sized piece of shale and the flint rock. He put the tip of the knife shale into the center of the dried moss and held it at a slight angle. Rowan then banged and scraped the flint rock on the knife slate downward toward the dried moss. Bright orange sparks flew at almost every hit and scrape, but the moss didn't even begin to smolder. *How the hell did Farr make it look so easy?!*

Frustrated and now missing his little friend, Rowan rocked back from his knees to his butt. He sighed and put his fire kit back in his pack for another time and retrieved the last of his food stores, the baked potato. Rowan ate the whole potato, skin and all. Barely filling up the void in his gut, it did, however, silence it. He laid out his cloak on his bed of needles, curled up in it like he did at the lake, and thought of his friends.

I bet Farr tried to come looking for me. I hope Maia had the sense to stop him. He can't be near me. I'm a target, and he would only get hurt again. I bet Maia is happy that I'm gone, not that she cared. She all but wanted me gone before that guy in black showed up. I'm sure Aislinn cried, but she and Luigh have their own path and new power. Power. Medeis. Why do I have it? Do I have it?? Fiiiirrrreeeee….

Rowan drifted off to sleep. Dreaming of fires. Fires in the hearths of Inns. Fires at the many campsites the group had shared. The fire in the village he destroyed. The fire in the dream with the man in the red mask.

The last part of the dream scared him awake. It felt like only minutes had passed, but Rowan guessed it must have been a few hours by the now risen full moon. He got up and stretched out his sore and stiff muscles. *At least it's a full moon. I can press on for a while.*

Rowan picked up his cloak and shook the pine needles off of it. He stuffed a hand full of dry needles in his pocket to add to his fire kit. *They make smoke a lot, but I'll be far enough away that no one will see.* He set off in his northwest direction up into the ever-increasing incline of the hills.

He acquired a large, mostly straight stick to help him with challenging steep terrain. *I'm glad winter decided to hold off, or this would most likely be impossible.*

After navigating a few crags and crevasses, Rowan came upon a small crystal-clear cool stream that he followed up the mountainside from a crevasse. The stream led to a placid clear pond with ice-blue clear water. He could see straight to the bottom of the rocky pond and saw a few schools of small fish swimming about. *Not big enough for a meal*, he sighed, and his tummy seemed to argue to the contrary. It was almost noon on the second day of his stealthy departure, and he was out of food.

Rowan looked around the pond and settled on a few Poplar trees on the opposite side to make his camp. Making his way over to them, he gathered a few long skinny branches, always on the lookout for a stick worthy enough to make a bow out of. Finding no such bow stick, he reached his goal for a campsite. Placing the long skinny sticks against one Poplar tree, he arranged them at almost a forty-five-degree angle from the ground to the tree trunk. He did this for every stick, at about three-foot intervals surrounding the tree. Rowan put his pack on the ground and took out some of his string. Using his sword, he cut six-inch pieces and made a slipknot noose on one end of each piece. He gathered the pieces of string and tied them to several places on each skinny stick. *At least my flight school survival training may come in handy for once.*

Rowan took a few steps back and admired his work. Finishing off the last of the water in his waterskin, he turned to the pond and went to refill it. The edge of the pond was mirror still, and it gave him pause as he looked upon himself in the reflection. He was dirty and grimy, his copper hair matted down on his head and forehead from his hood and sweat. He had black and brown dirt streaks on his cheeks. He looks down at his hands, dirt-caked under his fingernails, and numerous little scrapes and cuts on his dirty fingers. *What a sight I must be!*

He filled his waterskin, stripped down, and slowly waded into the cool water. He gave a short, shocking sound as he quickly inhaled when the water reached his waist. *Damn! That's cold!!* Rowan controlled his breathing as he stood naval deep in the water. Taking a deep breath, he plunged the rest of his body underwater. He shot back up and exhaled with a shiver. He did his best to scrub his hair and body without soap and longed for one of the copper tubs in the Inn he had made fun of. *That felt like another lifetime ago.*

Making his way back to shore, he shook as much water as he could out of his hair and used his dirty shirt as a towel. Rowan put the rest of his clothes on and walked back to his camp, rubbing his arms to try and warm himself back up.

He took a clean shirt out of his pack, put it on, and hung his dirty shirt on a branch of the tree he would sleep under. Rowan curled up in his cloak, still trying to control little shivers that racked his body now and then, and desperately tried to ignore the hole in his stomach. *Still not far enough away to safely make a fire if they did try and follow me. Oh, what I wouldn't give for a nice warm fire....in the common room....a nice.....roaring...fffiiirrreeeee.....and* sleep once again overtook him.

And he dreamt.

About fire.

A twig snapped!

Rowan awoke with a start at the sudden sound. His eyes quickly adjusted to the dusk light, and he saw it.

The lines.

Threads.

Coming out from him.

Crimson red and snow white.

Tiny thin threads, straight as an arrow.

Heat like a blast furnace welled up within him. Threatening to consume him. He mentally struggled against it, as sweat dripped from his forehead and off his nose.

The threads ran straight toward a stag. The crowned deer had stepped on a twig about twenty feet from where Rowan was sleeping. Its head turned toward Rowan, its eyes wide with the white of fear and shock, as it fell to the ground.

Rowan shook, not from the cold but with what he saw, and blinked. The red and white threads were gone, and the world seemed a little darker than it had been a moment ago. His breathing was fast with shock, and he was bone-chillingly cold again. Rowan closed his eyes and remembered his training to control his breaths and calm himself. Realizing he was on his knees, Rowan pushed himself up, opened his eyes, and saw the crumpled form of the deer. He had to will his feet to move, feeling like his boots were made out of cement.

As he approached the deer, he could see a two-inch diameter hole in its chest, right behind its shoulder. The hole ran straight through the deer, and the wound was cauterized. *What the actual frack was that!?!?!*

Rowan stared down at the deer for several minutes. He was shaken to his core by what had happened.

"Better start a fire." Came a gravely deep voice from behind him.

Rowan jumped and spun about, drawing his sword in a smooth motion. The steel of Rowan's sword met and bound with the steel of another, and Rowan felt like he had just attacked the rocky mountain face.

"Put that away before you hurt yourself, whelp," Angus said with his no-nonsense look.

Rowan relaxed the pressure he was applying to his sword to overpower the other blade, and Angus did the same. Rowan sheathed his sword, but Angus just held his. Rowan looked at Mr. Mountain and saw two things he had never seen before on the man's face when they sparred. A tiny bead of sweat and a glimmer of shock in his eyes. Not the shock of actually being afraid of something like heights, but a surprising shock as in facing an opponent with similar skill and strength.

"How'd you find me?" Rowan incredulously asked.

"You did well at first. It took me several hours to find where you departed from the road. It was easy after that. I caught up with you a few hours ago. Waited and watched. I could hear your stomach from yards away."

"Oh? Yeah. I'm starving."

"So you are. I had hoped that would make you turn back, but since you did this…" Angus said, pointing to the dead stag.

"Ah, yeah. About that…" Rowan sputtered.

"Yes. Tell me how you did that after you make a fire and I cook the meat for us both."

"Agreed."

Angus put his sword away and picked up the deer.

"After you." Angus motioned with the deer wrapped behind his head and on his shoulders.

Rowan looked at Mr. Mountain, nodded in affirmation, and made for his camp. *Wait! He stopped calling me whelp or boy!!!*

Chapter 15

Maia opened the door to the room and was pleased to see Aislinn, Luigh, Farr, and Damara still in it. The remaining group was split into pairs. Luigh and Aislinn were in the high-backed chairs, and Damara and Farr were sitting on the ends of the beds. All conversation had stopped the second Maia's hand was on the door's outer handle, but she did listen for a few seconds before she entered the room.

"...so by using Air and Water in an almost hexagonal pattern with the threads about 2cm in thickness..." Aislinn was telling Luigh.

"...then the 'bubble of silence' forms." Luigh finished Aislinn's sentence.

"I'm pretty sure," Aislinn said while confidently nodding her head.

"So, tell me about your thoughts on 'Healing'," Aislinn asked.

"Well, by taking Air, Water, and Fire down to the micrometer, possibly nanometer, and you visualize the cell organelles…" Luigh was saying and stopped abruptly when she heard the door handle to the room move.

All eyes were on her; Maia expected nothing less, demanded it by how she carried herself with confidence. She was a leader; even before her birth, it was her place in society, her noble heritage.

Maia looked at each one of them, *still fawns with the wolves gathering*, she thought and settled her gaze on Aislinn.

"Yes, child, you have worked out the *Dome* of Silence. Not a complicated weave, but usually reserved for Second Years," Maia turned her attention to Luigh, "and you, child, must not get ahead of yourself, and *never* let another Sister hear you speak in such a manner of *knowledge*."

"Why?" Luigh began stubbornly before adding the perfunctory, "Mother?"

Maia arched her eyebrow, "As I have told you before, the Yellows and Blues would lock you in a subbasement and pick your brain clean until you no longer can remember your name."

Luigh's eyes widened at the unspoken words that sounded very much like torture to her, "Ah, yes, Mother."

"Wait, if we would get *interrogated* for what we know, what about Farr???" Aislinn, suddenly realizing, blurted out.

Feeling defensive of her love, Damara got up and almost stood between Farr and Maia.

Maia held up a hand to Damara soothingly to show the Caitheness she meant no harm. "That is a bridge we will cross before we reach Occursum."

"I think, as our agreement, you owe us some insight into your *plan*," Luigh said, purposefully leaving off Maia's title.

Maia flatly stared at Luigh for two minutes, and Luigh sat up in her chair and returned the glare.

With an audible sigh and dropping of shoulders, Luigh resigned, "Mother."

With a very pleased look, Maia said, "Children, my agreement stands. My thoughts concerning Farr have been for him to remain with Damara and travel to her Woodland while you two train at the Spire."

"You never said how long the *training* lasts, *Mother*," Luigh replied.

"The average child trains for four years…"

"FOUR YEARS!" Luigh exclaimed while she shot up to her feet, almost knocking the chair onto its back. "We can't leave Rowan and Farr to who knows where, doing who knows what, for *four years*!"

"As I was saying, *child*, the *average* child takes four years. However, it has been done in as little as two and as long as six. The current Primus Princeps and I both graduated to full Sisters in three years of hard work and study. That is, for those that graduate."

Luigh stood in front of her chair, hands balled into fists at her waist, and was staring Maia down. Aislinn, recognizing Luigh's telltale body language of her about to fight, tried to intervene.

"What happens to the women that don't graduate?" Aislinn asked.

It was a question just curious enough to break Luigh from her laser beam lock on Maia, and she relaxed her fists but kept her hands firmly planted on her hips.

"Excellent question, child," Maia began, "When someone has the ability of Medeis but can not fully hold it, they are taught the basic control techniques I have shown you and sent home. The others that can not progress from one year to the next are either sent home, or given jobs in the Spire or Occursum proper depending on their level."

Luigh looked Maia straight in the eyes, "Do any runaway?"

Again, Maia flatly looked at Luigh and waited for her title.

The whole room waited, in silence so complete, it was deafening to hear each other breath. Damara slowly sat down next to Farr on the same bed, but all eyes were on Luigh and Maia.

Maia patiently waited while Luigh met her match for stubbornness.

Finally, after a few minutes, Luigh scoffed and muttered, "*mother.*"

Maia nodded, "All runaways are brought back to the Spire and face a disciplinary tribunal, made up of teachers in whatever year the child has accomplished or the Septem she had pledged. Now, go eat your noon meal and meet in my room at one for your afternoon lessons."

Maia didn't wait for any more questions to be asked. Instead, she quickly turned on her heels and strode out of the room. *I must be careful to strike the right balance of respect and stubbornness from her. She is the most powerful I've ever felt.*

When the door to the room closed, Luigh spun on the remaining three. "THAT WOMAN! GRRR!" she growled as she made tight fists with her hands again.

Aislinn stood up and put her hands on Luigh's shoulders. "That woman is from here and knows more than we still do," Aislinn said, trying to soothe Luigh.

"*For now*," Luigh growled as she relaxed her hands and broodingly sat down.

Aislinn, satisfied that Luigh wasn't going to go nuclear, turned to Damara and Farr, "What do you think of Maia's plan?"

Farr looked at Damara and she at him. "If she will take me, I will go with Damara," Farr said at Damara with a smile that split his diminutive face.

"We stay together, mo chridhe," Damara said, engulfing Farr's hand with hers, gently squeezing it.

Aislinn nodded at them and turned back to Luigh, "Well, at least we know where they will be, and they will be safe."

"I suppose," Luigh grumbled and shrugged her shoulders.

And they would give me *a hard time and call me moody!* Aislinn laughed in her head. "Anyone hungry?" she asked the room, smiling at the three of them.

Farr hopped off the end of the bed, followed by Damara simply standing up. "I could eat." He answered. Damara nodded at Aislinn, and Luigh huffed and begrudgingly stood up.

"Well?!?" Luigh said to them, "What are you all waiting for?"

Aislinn and Farr broke out in laughter, leaving Damara confused about not knowing Luigh as well as they did.

Luigh, Aislinn, Farr, and Damara left Rowan and Angus' room and went down into the common room to get some lunch. As they descended the main stairs from the second floor, they could hear that the common room was more full than it had been last night and even this morning at breakfast. Luigh recognized the armor most of the patrons were wearing as the Innkeeper met them at the bottom of the stairs. He waved at them to follow, weaving his way to a table almost in the middle of the room.

The group sat down on the hard pine benches on each side of the table.

"I feel surrounded," Aislinn whispered to Luigh.

"I think that's by design." Luigh hushly replied as she looked around at all the soldiers from Das Daingneach. "Let's keep the talk to the bare minimum." She told the table.

They let Aislinn do the ordering since she seemed to understand the serving girl the best. They were brought some sort of mutton stew with a hard wheat and oat bread. No water was offered; instead, they were all automatically given a stout ale. Farr took a sip of his ale, and Damara giggled at his foamy mustache. They ate in silence as the fighting men would occasionally break out in raucous laughter all around them. The group would look around every so often, but to Luigh, Aislinn and Damara, the men didn't seem interested in their table. Farr's sharp Lacerten eyes, however, saw what most missed. He caught the sly head pointing from one man to another in their direction or the quick sidelong glance from another. Farr was confident they were being watched.

Maia came in through the Inn's main front doors and walked straight up to the group's table. She didn't need any guesswork to find them; they stood out in the middle of the common room full of armored men.

"It is an hour past noon, children," Maia announced to them.

All four of them jumped a little in their seat as they hadn't known Maia even left the Inn.

The shock of Maia's approach to the table had Luigh forgetting her angst toward the woman.

"Yes, Mother." Luigh and Aislinn replied in unison.

Maia gave a curt nod and made for the main stairs to her room.

Luigh rolled her eyes after she realized she blindly just agreed to Maia. *Stupid woman*, she berated herself.

"Well, *Mother* beckons," Luigh said to the group as she pushed the bowl to the center of the table. "Come, Ais."

Aislinn looked at Farr and rolled her eyes, mocking Luigh. Farr had to compress his lips to keep from laughing.

"Shall we go about the town, love? I think I saw a bookstore." Farr asked Damara.

Aislinn followed Luigh up the stairs to Maia's door. Luigh reached her hand out to grab the handle and was suddenly thrown back in the air. Luigh's back thudded against the hallway wall opposite Maia's door, knocking the wind out of her. Luigh landed on the hallway floor on all fours, gasping for air.

Aislinn, instinctively, took hold of Medeis. Before she began to form and grab at the threads of power, she saw the glow of the threads on the door. *A test?* she wondered. Aislinn stepped past a still gasping eye-watered Luigh, gaining control of her breathing, and took a closer look at the weaving on the door. *Hmmm, looks like it's just Air. I wonder*, she thought as she reached out in the air with her right hand, as if she were picking at a speck of dust in the hallway air. Aislinn, holding Medeis, saw the tiny end of the weaving of Air on the door and pulled on it. The weaving quickly unraveled, and the thread of Air evaporated.

Aislinn watched the threads of Air go and then turned to Luigh, "Did you see that?"

Luigh stood up and brushed the dust off her dress, "See what?"

"There was a pattern of Air on the door. That must've been how you were knocked back. I pulled at the end of it, and it evaporated."

"What??" Luigh said, her brow and forehead furrowing.

"I'll explain later. We better go in." Aislinn said as she opened the door to Maia's room.

Maia was sitting in one of the high-backed chairs in her room, her hands folded neatly on her lap, smiling.

"Good work, child."

"Thank you, Mother," Aislinn said, feeling her cheeks flush with heat.

"That brings us to today's lesson. Weaves can be unraveled, but only the simple ones, and of them, mostly of the same element. When more than one element of Medeis is used, the unraveling can be…catastrophic. You can inadvertently form a pattern that is disastrous. Plus, I take it you now know a weave that is useful for guarding something?"

"Yes, Mother," Aislinn replied.

"I didn't see it, Mother," Luigh said, rubbing her back.

"I suspect not, child. You sprung the trap. Not to worry, I will show you how to weave it, and you will both practice the weave and unravel each other's."

"Yes, Mother," they answered in unison.

Maia got up and walked over to the small four-drawer pine dresser. She took hold of Medeis and began to weave the pattern she called 'Repulsio' on the top drawer. "Did you see now, child?" she asked Luigh.

Luigh nodded, "Yes, Mother."

"Good. Now, unravel it."

Luigh bit her upper lip and furrowed her brow as she tried to grab the tiny end of the weave. It took her several tries to grab hold, but it unraveled fast and evaporated once she did.

"Excellent, child." Maia praised. "The tighter the weave, the harder it will be to unravel. Luigh, protect the top drawer, Aislinn the bottom. When you have, let the other know and unravel them."

"Yes, Mother." came the unified response Maia expected.

Aislinn and Luigh practiced the repulsion weave and unravelling for almost four hours until it took mere seconds to do either function. When Maia saw that they had a good grasp of it, she interrupted them. "Very good, children. I believe it is time for supper. We will have a long day tomorrow, so I suggest you eat well and go to bed as early as you can. Move your stuff into Angus and Rowan's room, so you each have a bed to rest in."

"Yes, Mother," Aislinn said.

"But, Mother?" Luigh asked.

"Yes, child?"

"What if the weave is tied off in a knot?"

"That makes it more difficult to unravel, but not impossible."

"But, what if you folded the weave like you were tucking in a bedsheet?"

Maia's eyes widened in surprise, then regained her instructor composure.

"That can't be done, as far as I know, child."

Luigh furrowed her brow slightly in thought, then said, "Yes, Mother."

The three made their way down to the common room for supper, and the Innkeeper showed them to the same center table as they sat at for lunch. The room was once again full of the men from Das Daingneach. Maia smiled and proffered salutations to a soldier here and there on the way to the table. *Definitely, by design*, Luigh confirmed to herself.

They sat down at the table and saw that Farr and Damara were already there.

"What were you two up to today?" Aislinn asked them.

"We took a walk around the town," Farr answered. "We found a fletcher to replace a few arrows, a bookstore, and a shop that sold a pie made of a fruit called apples. It was delicious."

"Oh? Sounds good. Did you save any?"

"We did. We bought a pie for each of you."

"Oh, good! Thanks!" Aislinn said gratefully with a smile.

"What about you, Damara?" Maia asked. "Did you find any books to your liking?"

The whole table looked at Maia as if she sprouted five new heads with twelve eyes apiece.

"Um, no, unfortunately, all they had were the same main books about fables that my father already has," Damara replied.

"Ahh, pity," Maia said genuinely.

What the hell is up with this woman? Luigh thought, shaking her head in disbelief, *us she treats like actual children, but Damara and Farr she shows* actual *concern and interest? What the hell??*

The now smaller group reunited ate their supper of more mutton stew and wheat oat bread in silence. The general mood of the whole common room was more sober than at lunch. The military men's laughter was more subdued, if at all. They appeared to eat heartily and mill about with a sense of purpose, but no one left the common room.

"As I told Luigh and Aislinn, get as much rest as you can tonight. We leave at daybreak with Master Glenn and Lieutenant MacGill." Maia said to Farr and Damara. They nodded back in acknowledgment.

As they made their way to the main stairs, Maia again said a word here and there to an armored man; each man's hard and stern face melted by her words like a glacier feeling a spring sun.

The group went up the stairs and paired off to their rooms, while Maia had a room to herself. Farr and Damara said goodnight to Luigh and Aislinn, who returned the sentiment, but when the four turned to say the same to Maia, she had already gone into her room. *Typical*, Luigh said to herself.

With a final wave of goodnight, Luigh and Aislinn went into their room and closed the door.

"Do the bubble," Luigh commanded Aislinn.

Aislinn sighed, took hold of Medeis, and did the weave.

Luigh, holding Medeis herself, saw the weaving and nodded to herself in memorization.

"Good. I have an idea. Watch closely."

Luigh walked over to the small four-drawer dresser in their room and wove the repulsion. With her tongue slightly protruding the corner of her mouth, she made a motion as if she was tying a shoe, then gathered the ends of the threads and the knot. She made a flipping motion with her hands and a tucking.

"What the *hell* did you just *do*?! Aislinn exclaimed.

"I think I tucked the threads in. Did you see it?"

"IT DISAPPEARED!"

"What disappeared??"

"The WHOLE WEAVE!"

"Wait, what?! It's still there. You can't see it??"

"Nope!"

Luigh reached with her hands and untucked the knot and ends of the thread. She then deftly untied the knot, letting the ends of the threads dangle.

"How about now?"

"Yeah, I could see it once you *untucked* it."

"Fascinating!"

"What's *fascinating?*"

"Maia lied."

"I don't think she lied."

"If she didn't lie, then we know something she doesn't."

"We should show her."

"Like HELL I will, and neither will you!"

"Why?"

"This may be our only edge if we need to protect ourselves, or escape from her, the Spire, or who knows what else!"

"Ohhhhh. Yeah. I get it."

"Good. Now, you try. I want to see it disappear as well, and maybe we can see if we can uncover it too."

"OH! That's a good idea!"

Luigh and Aislinn took turns weaving the repulsion, tying it off, and tucking it in. When they each felt they had that down, they took turns feeling, fumbling, and starting to see a tucked-in weave. Aislinn was not as adept at untucking and untying as Luigh was, but she did manage to get it a few times before it got really late in the evening.

"Better undo the bubble weave before Maia finds it in the morning," Luigh said to Aislinn.

"Oh yeah," Aislinn said as she rolled out of bed and unraveled the weave. She blew out all but one half-burned candle in the room, leaving it lit so she could find her way back to bed.

"You could've used Air, silly."

Aislinn laughed, "I'm too beat to think about it."

"G'nite, Ais."

"Nite, Luigh."

Chapter 16

Morning came earlier than either Luigh and Aislinn expected or wanted. The incessant banging on the door finally woke them both.

"Ughhh," Aislinn groaned as she rolled over from her left to her right side.

"Go away!" Luigh commanded as she pulled the covers over her head.

Farr knew both of the women were notorious for waking up swinging, so he sent Damara in for the experience, giving her a slight warning, of course.

Damara opened the door to their room and strode in. Fortunately for Damara, her large size was mitigated by how lightly she stepped and barely made a sound on the pine slat flooring.

Heeding Farr's brief advice on how volatile they might wake, Damara shook Aislinn's feet to rouse her.

It only made Aislinn groan more and roll back onto her left side.

Damara decided to try Luigh and shook her feet. It was all Damara could do to take a step back as she felt the breeze and saw the blur of a blanketed foot sweep past her nose.

"I'mmm up!" came the reply from Luigh.

"Shhhhhh!" Aislinn said to the room.

"That's quite enough silliness from you two. Get on your feet now, or I'll dump the chamber pot on you both!" Damara annoyedly said as she slightly rubbed the end of her almost hit nose.

"Fine," Luigh said, sitting up and rubbing her eyes.

"Ugh, what time is it?" Aislinn groggily said, propping herself up on an elbow with one eye half-open.

"It's an hour 'till daybreak," Damara announced. "Hurry up and get ready if you want to fill your stomachs before we leave."

Damara waited until both Luigh and Aislinn had swung their legs over the sides of the bed and were at least sitting upright before she left the room.

"Ugh, you think they have coffee here?" Aislinn asked Luigh.

"Doubt it. Probably be more ale." Luigh quipped.

Aislinn chuckled at the image of how they seem to drink more ale in this northern area than anything else. Ale for breakfast, ale for lunch, ale for dinner, and ale whenever you're thirsty.

They both got to their feet and stretched, each taking turns using the wash basin, warming the water with Medeis, and gathering their clothes for the day. It was well-orchestrated, having spent quite a lot of time in cramped quarters, and this felt no different than the Novus.

Well, a bit different, Luigh remarked as she pulled on her riding dress over her tight-fitting moisture-wicking remnant of space travel. After they had both packed up all they owned on this world into two waterproofed leather packs, they walked out of the room without a second glance. Both more confident from their late-night practice, Aislinn in new skills, and Luigh in what she felt was an edge over Maia.

Down in the almost empty common room, Luigh and Aislinn could quickly locate Farr, Damara, and Maia at the center table. The absence of the soldiers and lack of sleep made the common room feel enormous to them, and it felt like they walked a quarter of a mile to the table.

"Good morning, children," Maia said as they approached, "I trust you slept well?"

Aislinn blushed slightly, wondering if Maia knew that they were up most of the night practicing. Luigh, however, felt confident.

"Like babies." Luigh sarcastically retorted.

"I see," Maia smiled, "My First Year, I think I averaged three hours a night. My roommate and I would be up past hours practicing everything we could. I suppose you are more disciplined than I."

Farr nearly choked on a dry piece of bread, and Damara gently patted his back.

"How'd you know??" Aislinn said breathlessly.

"Oh, child. We all start out the same way." Maia said motheringly. "I am impressed that you formed a dome of silence while you practiced, but you shouldn't do too many weaves at once. That's drawing too much Medeis at the same time."

"But I didn't." Aislinn said as she chewed on a piece of cheese, "I tied it off."

Luigh shot her a look of daggers.

Maia stopped, a cup of steaming tea in mid-raise to her mouth, and looked incredulously at Aislinn, "You did what??"

Aislinn swallowed the cheese hard, only having half chewed it.

"I, um, tied it…off?" Aislinn quietly said while trying to make herself as small as possible.

"That's impossible! No one has been able to do that since…well, for almost a millennium!" Maia said, her eyes wide in wonderment at Aislinn.

"Why?" Luigh scoffed, purposely leaving off 'Mother'.

Maia looked at Luigh and regained her composure almost as quickly as she lost it. She slowly sipped her tea, carefully deciding her following words and smoothing her raised eyebrows. "Well, child, no one has been strong enough with Medeis. In fact, some Blues theorize that the ability to use Medeis at all is dwindling. Perhaps due to the fact that male Medeis users are cut off from the ability, commit suicide, or are outright killed. There have been a few Blues that have advocated in starting a breeding program, but even most of their own Septem is against that."

Luigh realized that Maia had used the 'child' denotation and wouldn't get away without using the respectful 'Mother' again, for now. "I see, Mother. So, what you are saying is…"

"That you, child, and Aislinn may be the most powerful Medeis users since before the Breaking. But, always remember, children, that power alone is not the full measure of strength. Wisdom and skill are just as needed."

"Yes, Mother." came the unified reply.

"Good. Now finish up your breakfast quickly, children. We have a long ride ahead of us today. An army doesn't move as fast as a small group on horseback, or on foot for that matter."

The rest of breakfast went by quickly and silently, with Luigh occasionally looking up to see Maia looking back at her over a cup of tea. *Am I a threat to her now?* Luigh thought, *do I trust her more or less now??*

The group finished up, and Maia left a small pile of gold Occursum coins on the table. As they walked to the back bar area, Maia gave the Inn Keeper a few more gold coins, and they thanked each other. Leaving the Innkeeper at the front bar, they walked down the back hallway, past the kitchen and back stairs, through the back door, and into the alleyway to find their horses saddled, loaded, and waiting. Master Glenn was also there, on foot holding the reins of Maia's sandy blonde gelding.

"Good Morning, Mistress, um, Mary."

"Good Morning, Master Glenn." She replied, "Thank you." As she hoisted herself into the saddle and took the reins from him.

Glenn did the same for Aislinn, Farr, and Damara, and they each thanked him for the help. When he tried to help Luigh, she shot him a 'back off' look that made him take a step back and hold up his hands in surrender. Luigh gave a satisfied snort and hopped up into the saddle by herself.

Glenn put his hands on his armored waist and let out a chortle as he smiled.

"Thank you, Master Glenn," Luigh said, "but I got this."

"So you have," he replied, "Mistress Nighean. You would make an excellent bean ghaisgich."

Luigh raised an eyebrow and thought for a moment in translation. She could hear the snickering coming from Aislinn and Farr, then the translation came to her.

Looking sternly at Glenn, she said, "I am nobody's *warrior wife, especially yours*!"

Glenn laughed even more, "Oh no, Mistress! Not for me, you're too young for me," and he winked at her.

Luigh harumphed and sat up high in her saddle, her unbraided ponytail matching the swinging of her dark brown horse.

Aislinn and Farr couldn't hold it in any longer, and both doubled over in their saddles in laughter. Even Damara and Maia chuckled a little.

"We best be going, Master Glenn." Maia interrupted the joviality.

"As you wish, Mistress," Glenn said, his right hand on his left chest in salute, and he got into his saddle in full armor seamlessly, as he had been doing for almost his whole life.

They made their way out of the alleyway and to Mächtige Mauer Road, where they met up with the rest of the host from Das Daingneach. Maia introduced the group to Lieutenant MacGill. Everyone in the group except Damara raised their heads to look at him. Along with his hazel eyes, Luigh noticed that his brown hair was in the Northern Warrior style of shaved sides and a ponytail. His armor, as was the host's, was a dull gunmetal color that was well taken care of. The armor didn't reflect the light but was easily visible in the snowy climate of the North. He, as did Master Glenn, had a long sword on their backs at an angle, the handle in easy reach, and the butt end of the scabbard easily canted off to the side to allow for horseback. Farr noticed that the grip of both swords looked like Rowan's with a runic bird inlaid under the leather.

The sun was just starting its long rise, and the cicadas portend another hot day in what should've been late fall. Farr wondered how these men could stand being in full armor in these conditions. Damara saw his puzzled, concerned look. "It does get warm in the North during the summer, love. Plus, I'm sure they sometimes ride into the Vastante, which is much hotter than it is here."

"I suppose," Farr said, still looking at the men, "but that doesn't make it comfortable."

Damara chuckled, "ah, my love, you are very caring." As she reached out and caressed his arm. Farr looked away from the soldiers to her. He smiled with a hint of sadness in his eyes as he thought of his dead mentor, Llyr, and Rowan lost all alone somewhere to the North.

MacGill gave the order to ride, repeated by a much louder Glenn. It was repeated down the line's right-hand side. The group joined MacGill and Glenn in front of the host. MacGill in the middle, Glenn to his right, and Maia on his left. Farr, Damara, Aislinn, and Luigh rode behind the leaders, four abreast, and the host followed behind. The pace was set at a leisurely walk for the horses, as men on horseback in full armor would tire the horses out quickly for the distance they would want to cover.

The long column of a thousand northern warriors, a Quia, a Lacerten, a Caitheness, and two long-lost earthlings left West Fork Town, crossed the West Fork River, and entered Ventus on the Mächtige Mauer Road.

According to Master Glenn, they made good time eating lunch on the road and only stopped long enough to water the horses and relive themselves. They stopped at the second village they passed an hour after the sun had set. The only Inn in the village could only house twenty of the men, plus Maia's group. The rest of the men made camp on the south side of the village. They ate, slept, ate, and got back on the road a good hour before sunrise.

"We should pass the West Road by noon and stop at the next village by nightfall," Master Glenn was telling Farr, "The next day should see us through one more village and Mächtige Mauer by the day's end. Not much of a Capitol City, if you ask me. A few Inns and taverns, a big walled town, really. If it wasn't for the distance, it's surprising that Meridiem hasn't sacked it sooner."

Farr listened to Master Glenn attentively as he pointed out the different flora and fauna, mostly with disdain that it wasn't as lovely and as diverse as Parva Frater, but it helped Farr understand this world better. Damara also listened to Glenn, as she mostly read about this part of the continent in books. She, herself, had only briefly been here when Rowan and the others were transported by the Obelisk. There wasn't much new in what she had heard, but it was nice to put a real-life image to things she had only seen in a drawing or read as a detailed description. A few of those things that were only described, she had a blank book out that she journaled in, and attempted to sketch, the height and shape of sage brush, the thorns of a prickly pear, a clutch of pheasant eggs, seemingly endlessness of the landscape devoid of trees.

The army road past the well-traveled West Road. Luigh saw the road sign for Occursum.

"Um, *Mother*?" she asked, "Shouldn't we turn left?"

"No, child. We will continue on to Mächtige Mauer and reprovision and rest well there." Maia answered back without looking back at Luigh.

Luigh narrowed her eyes at Maia's back; *what are you going to get us into now?* she skeptically thought at Maia's back. She edged her horse closer to Aislinn's and whispered to her, "I don't trust this. She's leading us to trouble."

"I think we can handle it better now. Besides, it's better than going back to school." Aislinn winked at Luigh.

Luigh rolled her eyes, "True."

As they neared the last village in their journey, they felt the climate changing as the air was dryer, and the days grew even hotter, but the nights were just as cold as in the North. "Stay hydrated," Master Glenn cautioned, "The dry air will kill as fast as an arrow, for your sweat will evaporate before you even know you are sweating."

The army's pace had slowed somewhat since passing the West Road to conserve the horses, and the water breaks became more frequent, even though the bathroom breaks were the opposite. It was well past sunset when they reached the intended village, again too small for the army. Aislinn, Farr, Luigh, and Damara were all grateful that the Inn served water with the meals and slept hard that night, not realizing how much energy was sapped out of their bodies as fast as their perspiration off of their skin. Luigh and Aislinn wanted to take a bath and get the road dust off of them, but both were so tired after dinner that they fell asleep fully clothed, and they still had another full day of riding to go.

Before setting out on the final day, Master Glenn went down the line and made sure all waterskins were topped off and water barrels were loaded in the provision carts at the rear of the army column. Luigh, Aislinn, and Farr were grateful that he did because, by noon, half of the barrels were empty from refilling of waterskins. Glenn also rode up and down the line every half hour and made sure everyone was drinking. Every two hours, the army would stop, and he would personally watch as each person refilled their waterskin to make sure everyone was drinking. This necessary preventative measure against heat stroke and dehydration slowed the army even more, and they had to ride almost until midnight to reach their final destination, Mächtige Mauer.

Farr, with his superior eyesight, saw the walls of Capitol first. They were only twenty feet high, raked back at a slight angle, and seemed to be made of stone, brick, and clay. When they road through the North Gate, Farr saw that the walls were almost twenty feet thick at the base and ten feet wide at the top. The gates themselves were thick wood that Farr suspected were imported, as trees didn't seem to grow anywhere around here. The streets were paved with a hard brick, and as the army rode through the city, Farr could tell that it was laid out in a big square.

As the army rode down the Main Street, groups, or divisions, would split off and make for an Inn until the final division at the front of the column came to the last Inn. Farr could see the hand-painted sign of a stallion in mid-run on it.

From the little German Aislinn had taught him, Farr read the words under the sign 'Königslauf' to be 'King's Run'. Due to the late arrival, everyone was given some bread and cheese and shown their rooms.

Luigh and Aislinn slept in late the following day.

"What time…is it?" Luigh said in mid-yawn while wiping her eyes.

"Where are we?" Aislinn said as she sat up and looked around.

"I recall you saying it was called King's Run."

"No, I mean, look," Aislinn said to Luigh sweeping her hands for Luigh to take in the room.

Luigh finished rubbing her eyes and blinked them into focus. Her jaw dropped as her eyes looked over the room from one side to the other.

The room itself was three times the size of any of the Inns they had stayed in. In fact, it was bigger than their rooms at Das Daingneach, but to be fair, they were sharing this one. The wall to Luigh's left had two large picture windows separated by a wardrobe made of pine ornately carved with horses, a writing desk beneath each window, also made of pine and ornately carved with horses. The far wall had one large picture window with a couch, two high-backed plush chairs, and a long coffee table, all on a large carpet that had a landscape like what they had ridden through the past few days. The wall to her right had another wardrobe flanked on either side by eight-drawer dressers and a door that presumably led to the hallway. Luigh got up and looked at her four-posted canopied bed, made of pine and ornately carved with horses like all the furniture in the room. The sconces on all the walls were brass oil lamps set at three-foot intervals where possible, and there were two three-candle brass candelabras on each writing desk.

"Uh, now I understand the question." Luigh said to Aislinn, "Wow," and she let out a low whistle.

"I'm totally taking a bath!" Aislinn announced.

"Same! But, I think we should find something to eat first."

Aislinn's stomach grumbled in agreement.

Since they were still dressed, albeit wrinkled, they left their room and tried to retrace

their groggy steps from late last night. They
turned right out of their room and walked down
the hall, only passing one other door before they
found the main stairs. They went down them for
two flights and came out into the back end of the
common room, which to Aislinn and Luigh wasn't
so common. It was twice as ornate, with more
brass oil sconces, and brass oil chandeliers, two
massive cobble stone fireplaces, one in the center
of each wall, a double door on the third wall with
picture windows down the length of the wall, with
the final fourth wall being the bar/kitchen area.
The tables in the center were sturdy pine, as well
as the tongue-and-groove paneling on the walls.
A few hung oil paintings depicted various herds of
horses in the Ventus prairie landscape.

"Are you sure this is an *Inn*?" Luigh
asked Aislinn.

"Didn't you read the sign?" came a voice
behind Luigh, making her jump.

Luigh turned around and saw Maia
smiling; she was all clean and in a new purple
dress.

"Do you two need help finding the baths,
children?"

"Um, kinda, Mother." Aislinn sheepishly said, looking down at her dusty and dirty riding dress.

"There's one in the middle of each hallway, opposite the main stairs, child. Shall we eat first?"

"Yes, Mother, thank you," Aislinn said.

Luigh watched the whole conversation with a dower look on her face. *Of course, that woman would be up, clean, and in a new dress already. AND, she still placates us as if we were newborns!*

Instead of letting her thoughts out, Luigh bit her lip and followed Maia into the not-so-common room.

After the three of them finished their meals, lunch for Maia but breakfasts for Aislinn and Luigh, Maia cleared her throat and put her snow-white porcelain teacup down on its matching saucer.

"I'm sure your riding dresses have been worn out from our journey so far," Maia said as she doled out a pile of gold Occursum coins on the table. "This should be more than enough and perhaps a few arrows for you, Aislinn?"

"Yes, Mother, thank you," Aislinn said.

Luigh just looked at the pile and then at Maia. *And what price am I paying for now?* she thought, looking at the small pile of money. *She knows we are at her will not having money or a way to make any…yet.*

Luigh closed her eyes and swallowed her growing ire, "Thank you…Mother." She strained to eke out.

"You're quite welcome, children. Aislinn should have a decent grasp of the local language, but they know the common tongue well here. Since we are near the Palace, I'm sure you won't have any trouble finding reputable shopkeepers. We will remain here for two days, so make sure the dresses are ready tomorrow."

"Yes, Mother." Came the combined reply.

Maia nodded curtly, pleased that this wasn't a fight with Luigh, rose, and took a step away from the table. She paused and turned back to the table, "Oh, before I forget, be ready and at my room by four, tomorrow afternoon, in your best dresses. We have been invited to dine with the King. Your time is free until then."

Maia didn't wait to see both of their slack-jawed looks and continued walking away, back up the main stairs to her room on the second floor, smiling to herself at the last-minute directive. *Dinner isn't until six, so that should give me enough time to instruct them in court manners, tame their hair as well as Luigh's tongue.*

Luigh and Aislinn looked at each other, dumbstruck.

"Dinner?" Aislinn said.

"King?!" Luigh replied.

Luigh, with her elbows on the table, put her face in her hands. "And there's the bill due."

"Huh??" asked an even more confused Aislinn.

"Oh, nothing," mumbled Luigh. She raised her head and looked at Aislinn, "We best get going."

Luigh didn't wait for Aislinn to agree, and she got up from the table and started for the main door to leave the Inn. Aislinn had to quickly scoop the coins into her belt purse and hurry after Luigh, catching her at the entrance.

Luigh looked left and right down the wide brick sidewalk.

"Which way?" Luigh asked.

"I dunno, left??"

Luigh didn't reply but started walking in the direction Aislinn suggested.

Oh great, Aislinn thought, *I'm going to have to deal with hurricane Luigh all day. I hate when she gets this way! If she would only just decide on whether to just accept Maia's ways and realize what we can learn from her, or just have it out with her and go on her merry way! I, for one, am going to see how much and how far I can push this new power!!* Aislinn, lost in her thoughts, had to hurry up again to catch up with Luigh, who was almost a block ahead of her.

"…over there." Luigh was saying, pointing across the street at a shop that had dresses in the window. "Ais?" She looked around to see that Aislinn was ambling way behind her and had to run to catch up. Luigh rolled her eyes at Aislinn's absent-mindedness, but something behind Aislinn snapped her vision back. The sidewalk had many people going this way and that about their day, but there was one individual, a few people behind Aislinn, that was unmistakable in his attire. Gunmetal-colored armor with a white stag head on the chest, broad shoulders, a very noticeable scar on the left side of his face, and the sunlight bouncing off his bald head. *What the hell?!?* Luigh thought incredulously, *a babysitter*!!

Aislinn caught up to Luigh and noticed her scowling back down the sidewalk. "What's up?"

"Take a look," Luigh said, nodding her chin back down the sidewalk, "We have a shadow."

Aislinn looked back over her shoulder and saw him, Master Glenn, and broke out in a smile.

"Oh good!" she happily exclaimed, "He can help me pick out good arrows!"

Luigh rolled her eyes again; *I'm going to make myself dizzy with all this eye-rolling,* she laughingly thought. Luigh shook her head of the growing angst, put her hands on her waist, and said, "Well, let's wait for him to catch up then."

Aislinn waved her hand at Master Glenn, who stopped trying to sculk about in a lousy attempt to follow them. He took a deep breath, let it out, and continued to stride up to them.

"I guess I'm easy to spot here." He sarcastically joked.

"Indeed." Luigh acerbically shot back at him.

Master Glenn stopped dead in his tracts at Luigh's retort. "Um, ah, shall we??" he sputtered, offering his hand in the direction they were heading.

"Actually, we need to cross the street," Luigh said, pointing at the dressmaker's shop.

"Ahhh. I see, Mistress Nighean."

"Please call me Luigh."

"As you wish, Mistress Luigh."

Luigh shook her head at the older but still menacing-looking broad-shouldered man and chuckled.

Looking both ways, to be clear of any horses or horse-drawn wagons, Luigh lead them across the street and into the dressmaker's shop. A little bell attached to the door frame rang when the door opened. A corpulent woman, appearing to be in her mid-forties with blond hair streaked with grey, came out from a back room.

"Kann ich ihnen helfen, meine Damen?"

"Yes," replied Aislinn in common, "we require a riding dress, each please."

The woman looked the three of them up and down and raised an eyebrow at Master Glenn.

He laughed and held up his hands, "Oh no! Not I, my good Mistress."

Aislinn and Luigh looked at each other and chuckled when they both realized what Aislinn had said.

The dressmaker just nodded, "oh good. Please, Damen, come over to zee table and look at zee pattern books and svatch books. Ring zee bell vhen you are done." She said in a Germanic common accent. She led them to a small round table with four spindle chairs, all made of pine, with two large bound books on it. She went to a side counter and returned with a small handbell.

"Thank you," Aislinn said.

The dressmaker nodded and walked back through the curtain into the backroom.

Aislinn and Luigh sat down and started to look through the pattern book. Master Glenn tried to become part of a wall, very obviously not wanting to be there. After a few minutes, they found a riding dress pattern and, leaving the page open, switched to the swatch book.

After slowly flipping through the book, Luigh leaned close to Aislinn, "How long should we make our *babysitter* suffer?"

Aislinn giggled, "Awww, not too much longer. I rather like him."

Luigh broke out in laughter and looked over her shoulder at Glenn. He glared back at her, which made her laugh even more. Giggling in spurts while turning a few more pages, she nodded at Aislinn. Aislinn rang the little hand bell, and the dressmaker came back out into the showroom.

"You Damen have decided?"

"Yes. May we please have this pattern in these two materials?" Aislinn said, pointing to the open page in the pattern book and flipping between two pages in the swatch book.

"Ah, yes. Exzellent choices. I have zee material and know zee pattern vell. Very sturdy." The dressmaker measured Aislinn and Luigh with a tape measure. "I can have it ready by next veek."

Having gone through this in Baile Atha Cliath, Aislinn stuck her hand in her belt purse and pulled out a palm-full of coins. Luigh saw the woman's eyes widen at the sight of the gold coins.

"May we please have them by tomorrow morning, Herrin?" Aislinn asked, slowly putting a gold coin in her open palm one at a time.

When Aislinn reached nine coins, the dressmaker said, "As you vish, meine Dame."

Aislinn handed the dressmaker the money, and the dressmaker gave them a deep curtsy. Then, the three of them left the shop, and Luigh turned to Aislinn, "What was *that* about?"

"She thinks you are a visiting Lady," Glenn replied.

"Lady?" Luigh asked.

"Nobility." Glenn flatly said, looking down at Luigh.

"Oh, brother!" Luigh said exasperatedly.

Aislinn giggled as she recalled her recent youth pretending to be a princess.

Glenn picked up on Luigh's sarcasm and slight embarrassment, as well as Aislinn's elation, and said, "Where to now, My Ladies?" and he gave Aislinn a wink.

"I require arrows, my good Sir," Aislinn said, continuing the ruse.

"Right this way, My Little Lady," Glenn said and held out his arm for Aislinn to take. She put her arm through his, and he led her down the sidewalk to the right of the dressmaker's shop, leaving Luigh to stand there, flabbergasted.

"For crying out loud, you two!!" she yelled after them. She heard their guffaws and ran to catch up.

They walked another two blocks from the dressmaker and found a fletcher's shop. With the little doorbell ringing, they went in and were met with a young man in his thirties. He looked at Luigh and smiled. Glenn saw the fletcher's gaze and moved to stand in front of Luigh. The fletcher's eyes went wider as they went up to meet Glenn's; he swallowed hard and coughed out, "May…I help…you?"

"My Lady requires true hardwood broadhead tined 25-inch arrows."

"As you vish, Master…"

"Maighstir Armachd Glenn."

The fletcher's eyes were so wide they almost popped out of his head. He gave a squeak at Glenn's title and made a sweeping bow that made him look like he was about to tie his boots.

Glenn looked back at Aislinn and gave her a wink as he smiled at her. She started to giggle and put her hand to her mouth to stifle it.

Glenn turned back to the bowing fletcher. "Now." he boomed.

The fletcher almost fell over onto his face as he tried to get up fast and ran into the back room. After about five minutes, the fletcher came hurriedly back out. In a half bow, he held up his hands to Glenn and presented 30 arrows to Glenn's exact request. Glenn took his time and examined each one while the fletcher remained in his half-bow presentation. Satisfied, Glenn announced, "eight gold."

"A fair price, Maighstir Armachd Glenn."

Glenn reached his hand behind him, and Aislinn placed eight gold coins in it. Glenn paid the fletcher and took the arrows.

"Thank you, Maighstir Armachd Glenn. Please come back again, Maighstir Armachd Glenn." He said as he made another sweeping bow as the three left the shop.

Outside of the shop, Aislinn turned to Glenn, "That was fun!"

"Yes, but also rude. You will see tomorrow what I mean." Glenn said as he held up a cautioning finger.

"Like a newly made First Lieutenant dressing down a Private for failing to stand-to fast enough when he entered the room." Luigh correlated.

Glenn raised his bushy grey eyebrows in surprise, "Exactly, Mistress Luigh." He said with newfound respect.

"Ah," Aislinn replied to Luigh's example with understanding. "Time and place."

"Exactly." Glenn agreed. "Now, where to next?"

Luigh looked at Aislinn with a glint in her eye and a sly smile on her face. *Well, if I'm going to have a babysitter, I might as well have some fun!*

Aislinn saw the gleam in Luigh's eye and knew what it meant.

"To the bar!" they both exclaimed at the same time.

Initially taken aback at their brashness, Glenn grinned so much that it pulled the scar on the left side of his face. "To the tavern!" he said, pointing back the way they had come.

He led them back across the street and past the Inn for a block. Luigh and Aislinn heard it before they reached the doors, raucous laughter and the course language. They smiled at each other and followed Glenn into the Tavern he knew would be safely full of his men.

Chapter 17

A nother morning came earlier than either Luigh and Aislinn expected or wanted. Their heads pounding from whatever they had been drinking the night before.

"uuuuuuugggggghhhh," Luigh groaned, drool connecting her mouth to her sheets. Her horsehair-filled pillow was on the floor, along with her riding dress.

"ssssssshhhhhhhh," Aislinn responded, pulling her pillow over her head.

"What did Glenn call that stuff we were drinking?" Luigh quietly asked.

"Mead." Aislinn muffled from under her pillow.

"Remind me to never drink that."

"Agreed."

"Get up, Ais. We have to get our new riding dresses and come back and get ready for tonight."

"Ugh, do we have to?"

"Unfortunately. *Mother said so.*"

"Fine-a," Aislinn said as she begrudgingly pulled the pillow off of her face and squinted at the room to see a blurry Luigh slowly sitting up in her bed in only her moisture-wicking space clothes.

"Um, Luigh?" Aisling asked while pointing to Luigh, "Did anyone see you in that?"

Luigh looked at Aislinn, confused, then looked down at her clothing.

"Oh, ah, no," Luigh mumbled, "I stripped after Glenn walked us to the room.

"More like he *carried us* to our room."

Luigh started to laugh, remembering the image of Glenn carrying them both like a sack of potatoes under each arm, then held her head in pain. "Ugh, don't make me laugh."

"We need water and lots of it," Aislinn remarked.

"I could use acetaminophen," Luigh said.

"Oh yeah, even better."

"Wait…I have an idea." Luigh said, swinging her legs over the side of the bed toward Aislinn. "Come here. Give me your head."

Aislinn slowly moved to a sitting position mirroring Luigh and looked at her, all confused.

"Your head, give it to me for a minute," Luigh told her.

Aislinn bowed her head toward Luigh. Luigh put her hands on Aislinn's head, closed her eyes, and surrendered to Medeis. She felt the power all around her, filling her up with warmth and splendor. She struggled to focus with her hungover brain but managed to thin out a strand of Water until she imagined it to be microscopic. She slowly threaded it into Aislinn and made a small weave around her meninges. Aislinn gave a slight shudder and opened her eyes as Luigh removed her hands from Aislinn's head.

"What was that?! I feel fantastic!" Aislinn said much more aloud than before.

Luigh put her hand to her own head, "Shh, not so loud."

"Oops, sorry," Aislinn said sympathetically.

"I used Water, microscopic, tight weave in meninge layer," Luigh explained.

"Got it. Give me your head." Aislinn said knowingly.

Luigh bowed her head toward Aislinn, and Aislinn repeated the process on Luigh. Luigh shuddered and opened her eyes when Aislinn was done.

"Better than acetaminophen," Luigh said as she winked.

Aislinn let out a giggle. "See! Now, if you could just get past yourself and use Maia as you think she's using us."

Luigh cocked an eyebrow, "So, you are lecturing my behavior now?"

"Well, as I see it, she has some sort of grand plan for all of us, and I intend to pull every ounce of knowledge about Medeis from her as possible. Two years my ass, I'll graduate her Spire in one!"

Luigh laughed at Aislinn's bravado. "I'll do it in six months!"

"You're on!"

They shook hands and laughed.

"I suppose we should see what time it is and figure out if we should eat first or get our dresses," Luigh said as she stood up and stretched.

Aislinn looked out the closest window and saw that the sun was well above the rooftops but not yet at its zenith. "I'm guessing about ten or eleven-ish?"

"Dresses it is." Luigh determined as she picked up her dusty old riding dress.

"After you, My Lady," Aislinn said, making a sweeping bow sitting on the bed laughing.

Luigh shook her head with a half-smile and got dressed.

They made their way down to the common room and out of the Inn without seeing Maia, Farr, Damara, or Master Glenn. They walked back to the dressmaker's shop, with Luigh occasionally looking over her shoulder to see if Glenn was following them or they had a new shadow, but she didn't see anyone making furtive movements. Aislinn led the way into the shop, and Luigh followed her, giving one last look behind her. Satisfied they didn't have a chaperone, she closed the door to the shop. The dressmaker had already come out from the back room when Aislinn entered first.

"Ah yes, Damen. I'll be right back. Please vait a moment."

"Thank you," Aislinn told her.

The dressmaker disappeared behind the curtain that separated the backroom from the showroom for a few minutes, then came back out with the two new riding dresses.

"Vould you care to try zem on?" the dressmaker asked.

"Yes, please," Aislinn replied.

"You may use zis room." She said, showing them to what had first appeared to be a closet but turned out to be a small dressing room for one person at a time. It had a small wooden pine bench low against one wall, a double hook on the smaller back wall, and a full-length mirror on the wall opposite the bench.

"Oh good, thank you!" Aislinn happily said.

Aislinn went in first and closed the door. She was in there for about five minutes, then came out in her new riding dress and showed it off to Luigh. It was a deep purple, with silver embroidery in a knotwork pattern down the sleeves and encircling the cuffs, neckline, waist, and hem.

"Nice!" Luigh said.

"Why, thank you!" Aislinn said, smiling and giving Luigh a small curtsy. "Your turn!" Aislinn said as she gave Luigh a small push on her back toward the dressing room.

"Fine," Luigh said flatly, allowing herself to be prodded and herded into the small room. She was in there for about ten minutes before coming out in a pale-yellow dress with purple embroidery matching Aislinn's.

"Very pretty!" Aislinn said.

"Stow it!" Luigh said, feeling the heat rush to her cheeks. "Let's go eat."

Aislinn, with her old riding dress folded in her left arm, turned to the dressmaker and pressed a couple more gold coins in her hand as she said, "Thank you."

The dressmaker broke out in a wide grin, "Danka Damen!"

Luigh just nodded at the dressmaker as she folded up her old riding dress and tucked it under her left arm as she began to leave the shop. Aislinn followed behind Luigh, making their way back to the Inn for lunch.

They entered the Inn's common room and saw Farr, Damara, and Maia at the center table. Luigh let out an audible sigh, and Aislinn gave her a little shove from behind. Luigh stumbled a step forward and turned her head enough to shoot Aislinn a look, only to see Aislinn grinning behind her. Luigh and Aislinn made their way over to the table and joined them,

"…it was fascinating to see how it was constructed." Farr was telling Maia as Luigh and Aislinn sat down at the table.

"What was fascinating?" Luigh asked as she sat down, placing the folded up old riding dress on the bench beside her.

"Oh! Hi!" Farr said as he saw Aislinn and Luigh join them. "Damara and I got a tour of the city's walls. Very formidable, considering the landscape, materials, and technology. I was told that it could withstand a trebuchet even at its most narrow parts. I suppose our *friends* would even have a hard time at the thickest parts with their technology."

"Fascinating," Luigh said dryly, not at all interested.

Farr gave her a dower look, as he knew Luigh wasn't interested but fell for her verbal trap yet again.

"I see you have your new riding dresses, children," Maia said, taking in both Aislinn and Luigh's new appearance. She held up her right hand, and a young blond, blue-eyed, serving girl in twin braids came over from the bar. "Please take the girl's dresses to be laundered."

The serving girl gave a short curtsy to Maia and turned to Luigh and Aislinn with her arms out to take the old riding dresses. Luigh and Aislinn handed them over, and the serving girl gave them a small curtsy as well and disappeared down the hallway toward the kitchen.

"Thank you, Mother," Aislinn said.

"Um, yeah, thanks…Mother." Luigh mumbled.

Maia smiled at them in a motherly way. *Amazing. I've never felt this connection to any other student, even though these two were just a means to an end. Surprising that these three would be with the Phoenix. With Rowan. I knew there would be four, but I had not even considered the strength of the other three. He will need them, and it is up to me to mold them. The enemy is probing us, looking for Rowan, testing us all. I just hope there is enough time.*

"We have not ordered. Are you two up to eating yet?" Maia asked Aislinn and Luigh.

"And why would that be, *Mother*?" Luigh skeptically asked.

"Mead can be quite arduous when taken in large quantities, child."

Luigh narrowed her eyes at Maia, "Oh no, we are both quite well and hungry."

Maia's eyes opened slightly, and if one didn't look closely, wouldn't have seen the surprise on her face.

"Then, by all means, let us eat, children," Maia said as she rose her hand again, and another young blond, blue-eyed serving girl came to take their lunch order.

They finished their meal with minimal conversation as Maia was studying Luigh and Aislinn at their apparent quick recovery from what should've been a massive hangover. With Damara's continued advice on the subject, Farr was wise enough now to stay out of Quia business. Luigh reveled in the fact that she is making leaps and bounds past what Maia has doled out. Aislinn, feeling like she was standing on a bouncing betty, looked nervously from Luigh to Maia, but kept her mouth shut.

Maia finished the last sip of her tea and rose from her bench; being at the end and next to Farr was an easy task to slip out from the bench.

"I will see you all in my room at four, ready for the dinner, children," and she left without waiting for a response.

Luigh waited until Maia was well up the stairs, "*Do* you *believe* the *nerve* of that *woman!*" she said, seething through her teeth.

Farr and Damara also knew to stay well away from Luigh when she was in a mood. But Aislinn, somewhat unaware of how Luigh had asked, answered, "What do you mean?"

"She knew *what* we were doing, and I bet you *with* whom we were doing it!"

"Oh…" Aislinn said, realizing the pit of vipers she had just jumped into with both feet and the bouncing betty she was standing on just blew her legs off.

"AND," Luigh began whirling on Aislinn, "she also suspects our quick recovery!"

"I don't think…" Aislinn started to say.

"Oh *yes*, she does!" Luigh interrupted, "Didn't you see how she stared at us all through lunch!?!"

"Well, I was too busy…"

"Didn't you see, Farr? Damara?" Luigh interrupted Aislinn again.

Farr and Damara both held up their hands, clearly not wanting to get involved.

"We really should, ah, get going to, ah, get ready, sorry, Luigh," Farr said as he slipped off the bench and stood up, with Damara following him.

Luigh let out a puff of held breath in disgust and looked at Aislinn.

"Well?!?" she demanded.

"Look, Luigh," Aislinn began trying to smooth Luigh's feathers, "we already knew Maia was keeping an eye on us with Master Glenn. As to our hangover recovery, let her wonder. It's our little secret."

Luigh thinned her lips at Aislinn.

Aislinn smiled and winked at Luigh.

Luigh rolled her eyes, "I suppose one more secret against *her* is a good thing. Stars above, we know she has a ton of her own."

"Yup." Aislinn agreed, "Let's go get ready for the ball."

"Fine-a," Luigh huffed and got up from the table.

The pair went back to their room on the third floor, making a mental note of where the bathtub room was. They each grabbed a large terrycloth towel and soap they found near the wash basin in their room, grabbed robes that Aislinn had noticed were in the wardrobes and made their way to the bathroom. They didn't bother using the heated water in the big copper barrels but used Medeis instead to gently warm their baths.

"Ahhhh, I soooo needed this," Luigh said as she sunk down into the tepid water with a bar of soap and a washcloth.

Aislinn also made satisfying groans as she slipped into her bath.

They enjoyed the soothing warm water for a while, reheating with Medeis when the water began to cool, then began scrubbing the dust off their exposed skin and hair. After they felt clean enough, they both got out and washed their moisture-wicking clothes and underwear in the remaining bath water. They dried off, wrapped their hair in the towels like they were wearing turbines, and donned their cozy robes. Luigh and Aislinn gathered up their space clothing, wringing them out into the now dingy tub water, and carefully balled them up, so they would be nondescript. They went back to their room, hung their hand-washed clothing on the top rung of the canopy beds, and Aislinn used Air and Fire to gently dry out their damp clothing.

Satisfied, Aislinn gave Luigh a curt nod, and they both redressed in their space undergarments.

"What should we do about our hair?" Aislinn asked.

"I think braids will be sufficient."

They braided each other's hair and donned the fancy dresses they had made in Baile

Atha Cliath; Luigh's yellow silk with a blue floral pattern, and Aislinn's periwinkle silk with a purple thistle pattern. By the time they felt ready, a knock came at the door.

"Come," Luigh commanded.

The door opened, and Farr poked his head in, "Ready?"

"As we'll ever be," Luigh told him.

They went out into the hallway and saw the little Lacerten in a brown five-silver-button vest gilded in silver scrollwork at all the seams. A white puffy-sleeved silk shirt loosely tied at the neck poked out of the vest, forest green breeches, and brown leather boots that came up to mid-shin with silver buckles up the outside edges. He did a little pirouette in the hallway, his tightly braided hair held in place with the hair tie he had from Llyr, and flashed a big grin with his arms out at his sides.

"Well? What do you think?" he asked them, "Damara picked it out yesterday."

"You look smashing!" Aislinn said, returning his smile.

"Yes," Luigh agreed, "Very handsome."

"You both look beautiful as well, but wait till you see Damara!" He said as his tilted jeweleled eyes flashed.

Aislinn and Luigh chuckled at Farr's exuberance. "Well then," Luigh said with a rare smile, "Let's go see!"

The three of them made their way down to the second floor and to Maia's room. Farr led the way since he knew where Maia's room was. He knocked softly on the door, and they heard a response from within, "Come in, children."

Farr opened the door wide, and they entered Maia's room.

The room was similar to Aislinn and Luigh's in size and opulence, but with only one large king-sized bed. Maia and Damara were sitting in the living room area in the high-backed plush chairs.

"Ah, my love, let me look at you again!" Farr said as he walked into the room, seemingly to float on air towards Damara.

"Shhh," Damara said as she blushed, you'll embarrass me, mo chridhe."

Aislinn and Luigh saw that Damara was wearing a simple forest green silk dress with silver scrollwork that matched Farr's vest, and Maia was wearing a purple silk dress with a high neckline with white lace at the neck and sleeve cuffs. Maia's hair was a complex intertwining of braids pulled back and hung down her back.

"Sit, children," Maia said to Aislinn and Luigh, "Damara is very deft in braiding."

Damara blushed again at Maia's compliment as she got up.

Luigh and Aislinn sat on the edge of the coffee table as Damara went to work unbraiding their hair and re-braiding in an intricate knotwork. Holding each hairstyle with a Celtic knotwork hair needle and collar that Maia furnished, Aislinn's made of silver, and Luigh's made of gold.

Maia looked at Luigh and Aislinn as she made a few trips around the coffee table.

"Yes," she agreed to herself, "no facial paint will be needed."

"Makeup?" Aislinn whispered to Luigh.

Luigh just shrugged her shoulders.

Maia looked out of the window at the setting sun over the western roofs.

"Our escort should be here soon," Maia announced.

They didn't have long to wait before a wrapping came at Maia's door.

"Enter." She said with authority.

Lieutenant MacGill and Master Glenn entered the room, evident that their armor had been cleaned and polished. However, neither were armed, at least where Aislinn, Luigh, and Farr saw.

"By your leave, Maia Quia." MacGill said, making a slight bow.

"Yes, Leifteanant." Maia said, making a small curtsy, "We are ready."

MacGill straightened out and led the way out of the room. Maia followed him, with Luigh, Aislinn, Damara, and Farr. Glenn would take the rear of the procession. As Aislinn passed Glenn, he leaned down close and whispered, "Gle bhoidheach." Aislinn blushed at his compliment.

They made their way, single file, out of the Inn, turned right, walked two blocks, then turned right again, walked three blocks, and stopped in front of a massive gate that blocked the whole street. There wasn't much in the way of people walking around in the few blocks they had travelled since it was near dinner time and how apparently close they were to the palace. Aislinn, Luigh, Farr, and Damara had failed to look up when they approached to see just how big the gate was or the surrounding walls. MacGill was stopped at the gate by two armored Ventus guards, with the runic horse on their breast plates, and Glenn left the rear of their procession to join MacGill. Aislinn, Luigh, Far, and Damara saw both MacGill and Glenn produce a long knife from somewhere on their bodies and place them into the tops of their right boots. The guards nodded at MacGill and Glenn, then opened the righthand side big black iron gate.

The gate opened without a sound, obviously well oiled. As the group walked through the gate, Farr looked up and saw that the dark red-brick walls were as thick as the outer city walls, but this gate was complete with murder holes.

They emerged from the gatehouse and into a large courtyard with brick paths that twisted and turned, interconnected, all around poplar trees and small gardens; all leaves brown or fallen by this time near late fall and grasses a golden honey blonde straw color. At the far end of the courtyard, the group could see the five-story square bastion of a palace, no higher than any other building in the capitol. Made of the same dark red brick as the walls, the palace was not ornate but looked instead for function to Farr; *similar to Parva Frater,* he thought, *although lacking the mountain height, this one is short and squat to withstand bombardment.* There was only a single large flag draped above the entrance, but below the bastion's inner walls, like a giant tapestry, green with a large bronze runic horse in the center.

As the group made their way through the winding walkways in the courtyard, Farr and Damara noticed the guards strategically placed and spaced out along the top of the bastion's walls, almost blending in with the wall itself. Two liveried servants in tunics that matched the red brick walls with the bronze runic horse on their chests opened the two oversized thick pine doors with black iron hinges. They bowed as the group walked up the three steps to the entrance. Another servant in an off-white tunic and bronze runic horse on his chest was waiting just inside the entrance for the group. He made a sweeping bow and started to walk down the dimly lit grand hallway, beckoning MacGill and the group to follow.

Farr saw that the grand hallway had the potential for more illumination, but only half of the oil lamps were lit. *Interesting,* he thought as he pondered why. While lost in thought and blindly following Damara, he failed to see the many tapestries depicting armored men on horseback in reddish-brown armor and long lances in various states of warfare. Several doors led off to the right and left, but it was the large, well-oiled maple doors, so that they almost looked a dark oak, with iron hinges and braces that they were being led toward.

Another servant was waiting at the large maple doors for the group to be handed off. He was more ornately dressed in a red brick-colored vest with a bronze runic horse split by bronze buttons, a puffy off-white silk shirt, tight riding red brick breeches, and black riding boots polished to a mirror shine. He held a maple staff carved to look like a giant riding crop, with a runic horse carved at the top and the bottom tipped in bronze. He inclined his head at MacGill and Glenn, who returned the gesture. The herald then wrapped three times on the door with his big riding crop. The large right door opened, and the herald banged the giant riding crop on the floor three times and loudly announced, "Maia Quia, Leifteanant MacGill, Maighstir Glenn, Luighseach Nighean, Aislinn Inion, Fearghal, and Damara."

MacGill nodded again at the herald and led the group into the city block long and expansive throne room. Luigh, Aislinn, Farr, and Damara's heads swiveled back and forth as they were led into the throne room.

Six massive chandeliers held by thick black iron chains hung from the flat redbrick ceiling, holding twelve oil lamps apiece, were evenly spaced in two rows. Farr could see a bronze pipe running from the chandeliers up along the chain to the ceiling, over to the closest wall, and down to large bronze barrels. He saw a knob about a meter up the pipe from the top of the barrel. *Hmmm*, he hypothesized, *the knob is a regulator of the lamps, but is it restricting the oil, or does it move the wicks? If it does move the wicks, then they must be one wick split twelve ways at the chandelier, and if so, how do they overcome the capillary action necessary to travel so far? Fascinating.*

As Farr was lost in thought about the illumination, Aislinn, Luigh, and Damara were impressed by the other things they saw. Twelve large bronze braziers along the right and left wall, and at the end of the cavernous room, a five-step semi-circle dark red brick dais with bronze accents along the leading edges of the stepped dais flanked by two more massive braziers that made the other twelve look like matchsticks. In addition, a giant tapestry hung on the wall behind the dais that took up most of the wall, depicting a plethora of dark armored men on horseback in a full galloping charge in a massive triangle formation on a vast prairie. All had long lances facing down in their charge, except one. The second horseman in the front held a large flag on his long upright lance. The flag they had seen when they entered the bastion; a bronze runic horse on a field of green. The lead horseman was obviously a king with a bronze crown on his armored head. Luigh squinted a little at the tapestry. Even though it was humongous, she had to strain to see the flowing hair coming from the backs of all the helmets. *Is everyone here blond??* She sarcastically asked herself.

Apart from the dais, the colossal tapestry, and all the illumination devices, the throne room was absent of all other furnishings, save one. The group was being led by MacGill to a large, long maple table that could easily seat twenty people comfortably. There were no candelabras on the table, none were needed, and it was set for a full service for twelve. Aislinn noticed the matching dishes were all bone white with a bronze line encircling every dish, culminating in a bronze runic horse in the twelve o'clock position. The flatware was all bronze, with the same runic horse at the end of each handle. At the head of the table regally stood an armored man in his mid-forties, athletically built, blond, blue-eyed, clean-shaven, and stood about 6'2", obviously the King. To his right, a handsome petite woman in a bronze silk dress outlined with dark red lace at her sleeve cuffs and high neckline; she looked similar in age to the King, also blond, braided down her back in an intricate runic pattern, with blue eyes and stood up to his shoulder in height. Three armored men stood pencil straight and obviously military men to her right. The first man was clean-shaven, had black hair with hazel eyes, stood almost as tall as the King, and looked to be in his early 40s. The man in the middle was shorter than the first but taller than the woman, slightly more muscular than the other Ventus men present, and looked about his mid-thirties with blond hair and blue eyes. The last man was also athletically built, standing almost equal to the King; he had brown hair and blue eyes and looked the same age as the man in the middle. Being clean-shaven seemed to be the trend here, as all the men were, along with short-cut hair. All of them were standing behind their respective seats at the grandly set table.

When the group's procession arrived on the opposite side of the table from the woman and obvious high-ranking soldiers, the King spoke in the common tongue with a tiny hint of a Germanic accent, "Hail, and vell met! I am König Vilhelm Fuchs III." He swept his arm to his right, "and may I present, Königin Greta Fuchs,

Hauptmann der Pferdegarde Karl Grüber, Leutnant der Pferdegarde Stefan Müller, and Meister der Pferdegarde Hans Bracke." Königin Greta smiled and inclined her head when she was named, and the three military men clicked their heels, making a sharp metallic cracking sound that echoed throughout the throne room as they inclined their heads.

Maia walked around MacGill toward King Fuchs, "Hail and well met König Fuchs. May I present Luighseach Nighean, Aislinn Inion, Fearghal, Damara, Leifteanant MacGill, and Maighstir Glenn of Parva Frater." Luigh picked up on the order of the names and tugged at Aislinn's sleeve for her to follow as she walked around MacGill to join Maia. Damara had to do the same to Farr, as he was still engrossed in the chandelier setup. MacGill and Glenn also took the hint and arranged themselves behind seats accordingly. *Interestingly odd,* Luigh thought, *that Maia would not introduce herself. She must know this King Fuchs. I wonder why she is okay to be here and Parva Frater, but not Baile Atha Cliath? I wonder where else on this 'Continent' she is not comfortable??*

"Vunderbar!" the King said, smiling and rubbing his hands together, "Let us dispense vith the pomp and circumstance and eat. I just vish it vas under better circumstances."

Everyone took their seats. Luigh, Aislinn, and Farr were not unaccustomed to multiple serving dinners. Damara, however, was used to much simpler meals and needed a bit of coaching by Farr. The first three courses involved a lot of small talk of their travel, the weather, and news from other Kingdoms. The King accepted that Luigh, Aislinn, and Far were from Parva Frater, which satisfied Maia. However, the fact that Damara was from the Woodland near Baile Atha Cliath made a few eyebrows rise.

"Do you feel the Longing yet?" Queen Greta asked.

"Vhy are you travelling so far?" Grüber pried.

"I was on my way to visit family in Occursum with Maia Quia and was slightly detoured when we heard of your plight by Master Glenn. As for the Longing, it can take years to manifest, and I have not been long from a Woodland." Damara deftly handled the questions, again to Maia's satisfaction of not revealing their haphazard travelling and discovery of an abandoned Woodland not far to the Northwest from Mächtige Mauer.

After they had all finished their main course, the King sat back in the highbacked maple chair, heavily carved with horses, and announced, "and nov, the unpleasant business that has brought you all here. As you knov, our scouts report of a host of about 2000 cavalry have crossed into Ventus from Meridiem a little over a month ago. They have sacked and razed every village and town to ash as they march North to Mächtige Mauer. The Great Var may be a thousand years past, but it is still fresh on our minds here. This *invasion* is different, hovever. A King does not lead the host but a man. A man that can vield *Medeis*." King Fuchs said the last sentence, looking at Maia, steepled his hands, fingertips to his lips, and waited.

Maia casually and delicately wiped her mouth with her ivory-colored napkin, then replaced it on her lap, taking her time to evenly spread it out. Finally, she looked up at the King and gave a small soothing smile. "Your Majesty, I am aware of the man *possibly* using Medeis, and I know a Conclave has been dispatched from Occursum to deal with that *possible* threat. They should be here in Mächtige Mauer within three or four days hence. When they arrive, I suggest we combine our forces and meet this host."

"Three days vay be a day too late." interrupted Master Bracke.

King Fuchs held up a hand to forestall more objections from his side of the table. "I agree, Meister Bracke." He looked back over at Maia and leaned toward her, putting his elbows on the table, intertwining his fingers, "Maia Quia, our scouts do report the use of Medeis. They also report four Quia *vith* the man in question. *Your Conclave vill arrive too late.*"

Maia's eyes widened when she heard that four of her sisters were part of this invasion and apparently helping this man use Medeis. She regained her composure, negotiation was never her strong suit, but she had an established report with King Fuchs and intended to use all of it she could, "Your Majesty, I am at your service as well as my two students. Luigh is an adept healer, and Aislinn can aid in some offensive Medeis and is an accomplished archer. Master Farr has no equal, save his mate, Damara, as a scout and archer. What is your battle plan?"

The King slapped his hands flat on the table, making plates and bronze flatware bounce and rattle. "HA!" he shouted with a big grin on his face, "CLEAR ZE TABLE AND BRING ZEE MAP!"

A bevy of liveried servants hastily cleared the table, and the herald brought a long rolled-up parchment to the King. Fuchs flung the parchment out slightly above the table, holding the edge of it, and unfurled a map of Mächtige Mauer and the surrounding area. Bracke and Müller placed small weights on the four corners. King Fuchs pointed to a flat plain a league south of Mächtige Mauer. "Here. This is vhere ve shall meet the enemy."

Aislinn, Farr, and Damara leaned forward in their chairs, watched, and listened intently as the King laid out his battle plan. MacGill, Glenn, and Maia added, subtracted, and made suggestions with rebuttals and agreements from Bracke, Müller, Grüber, and King Fuchs. Luigh just sat back, her mouth agape in horror at being conscripted in a war that was not hers, on a planet that she didn't come from. The more they spoke of battle, the angrier Luigh became, until she began to visibly start shaking, hands balled into fists. She was about to burst, and Aislinn caught on.

"Shhhh," Aislinn whispered to Luigh, putting a hand on her left thigh in an attempt to calm Luigh, "not now. Wait till we can get Maia alone."

Luigh shot Aislinn a look she had never seen before and was physically taken aback in terror, carefully removing her hand from Luigh's leg slowly as if backing away from a coiled pit viper about to strike. Sure, she has seen Luigh frustrated, mad, even angry occasionally, but this was pure, white-hot rage.

The planners had finished, all in a compromising agreement about what they thought was the best battle plan that would allow enough time for the Conclave to arrive and win the day. Aislinn missed the final agreed plan but caught the gist of what her role was going to be; stay with Maia. Luigh completely missed the whole plan, lost in her growing fury.

"Vell," the King announced to the table, "now that that's settled. Please enjoy your stay in Mächtige Mauer, but get plenty of rest. Ve vill gather our host at the South Gate a day hence." The King stood up, and everyone did as well. He held out his arm for Greta, and the pair made for one of the side doors in the throne room. Bracke, Müller, Grüber did their heel-clicking and head inclining again and made for a different side door than the King and Queen exited.

Maia looked from Damara to Farr, Aislinn, and then Luigh. She saw the raging fire seething in Luigh's narrow eyes and calmly addressed the remaining group while still looking at Luigh, "Let's go, children."

MacGill led their procession back to the Inn. He and Glenn said their goodnights in the grand common room and left for their Inn. Maia still saw that Luigh's ire was not abated from their short walk. "Get rest, children," she said and walked away before Luigh had a chance to blow.

Luigh let out a low growl at Maia's back. Damara was about to put a hand on Luigh's shoulder when Farr stopped her, shaking his head 'no'. Luigh couldn't stand it anymore and stormed off, going up the main stairs to the rooms above. Aislinn and Farr looked at one another.

"Should we follow?" Farr dared ask.

"I think we should. It might come to blows. I've never seen her this mad." Aislinn said. "Ever."

They started to walk to the main stairs, and just as Aislinn placed her foot on the first step, they heard a loud bang and crash, like a tree exploding from its sap freezing in sudden subzero temperatures. They started to run up the stairs, Farr quickly outstripping Aislinn and Damara with his Lacerten agility and speed.

Farr leaped up the stairs, two at a time, nimbly turning and pushing off one foot on the landing to the next flight of stairs to the second floor. He knew the loud noise was no coincidence, planted his right foot, absorbing the sudden stop by bending his right knee, and used it to push off to his left and propel him down the hallway. He slid to a halt just before Maia's room and saw that the door was missing. He flattened himself against the wall by the door jam and quickly looked into the room.

At first glance, he saw that the door to Maia's room had burst inward, Luigh standing amongst the remnants of the splintered wooden door, her back to the now open doorway. Farr took a deep breath and took a step into Maia's room with his hands up.

"Luigh?" he quietly said.

She quickly turned her head to look at him, making him stop in his tracks. He could see her left hand raised out in front of her and Maia calmly floating a good foot off the ground.

"Stay out of this, Farr!" Luigh hissed. "This is between me and *her*!"

Aislinn and Damara caught up to Farr and stood to either side of him, just inside the doorway.

"Please, Luigh." Aislinn pleaded. "Not this way."

Aislinn squinted and reflexively held up a hand against the bright glow of Medeis surrounding Luigh. She could feel that Luigh was even stronger than she was.

"Luigh." Maia softly said, standing midair with her arms tightly against her sides. "We can talk about this calmly."

Luigh's head turned back at Maia so fast her hair whipped around and almost whipped her own face.

"NO! I'm done listening to YOU! You're a MANIPULATOR and a LIAR!" Luigh barked.

"I have not told an untruth, Luigh." Maia calmly said.

"Please, Luigh, we still need her," Aislinn begged.

"*WE* do not need her," Luigh said over her shoulder, "*SHE* needs *US*!"

"We need each other." Maia proffered.

Luigh's eye's narrowed, and she started to make a grasping gesture with her outstretched left hand at Maia. Maia's eyebrows raised slightly, and her mouth opened as if she was about to exhale.

Luigh closed her eyes, waving her left hand dismissively, and Maia fell the foot to the ground, falling to her knees and left hand. Maia used her right hand to rub her throat.

"…fine," Luigh said as she turned on her heels and pushed past Aislinn and Farr. "I need some air."

Aislinn rushed over to help Maia up as Farr and Damara watched Luigh walk down the hallway, with her head held high, and down the main stairs.

"Should we follow?" Damara asked Farr.

"I would advise against that." Farr said, pointing to the once whole door, "considering."

Damara nodded in understanding. *Never involve yourself in Quia matters*, she thought, remembering her father's sage advice.

Maia slowly got to her feet, with Aislinn's help, still gently rubbing her throat.

"I think that we will be able to talk somewhat more rationally, now that that is out of the way," Maia said a little hoarsely, looking at the opening to the hallway. Then, she looked at Aislinn, "Be a dear, and bring me some water, child?"

"Yes, Mother."

Maia waved Farr and Damara to come further into the room and sit in the living room section. She sat in one of the high-backed chairs and took the glass of water from Aislinn. She took a sip and coughed slightly. "Thank you, child. Please have a seat."

When the three of them had sat down, and she had drunk almost half of the glass, she asked Aislinn and Farr, "On a scale of one to ten, how angry was that?"

Farr and Aislinn looked at each other with apprehension before they unanimously answered, "Ten."

"Good."

"Good?" Aislinn asked.

"Yes, I needed to know her breaking point."

"Why on Proximus would you even try and do that?!" Aislinn asked incredulously.

"You see, child, for what I fear to come."

"I don't understand. The battle?"

"This will be all but a skirmish in a much bigger war, child."

"But, Mother, it's not *our* war."

"As long as you are on this planet, it is *everyone's* war. It will be fought in the sky, on land, in the water. There will be nowhere to hide."

"The ground will shake. The sky will shatter. Nowhere to hide. It will not matter. The Phoenix will fight. It will be his might. The Basilisk will fall. To conquer no more." Farr said, his eyes closed, reciting from memory.

"The Prophecies?" Damara asked, looking at Farr quizzically.

"The Prophecies," Maia said matter of factly and gave Farr a small smile. *That one is full of surprises*, she thought fondly at him.

"Well," Maia started while standing up, "I suggest you all go to your rooms and get some rest." She turned to Aislinn, "Please come here tomorrow after breakfast. I have some lessons for you to prepare for the battle. Luigh may join us, if she wants. Now, to see about getting this room cleaned and a new door." Maia said with the last with a bit of chuckle.

Maia's sudden jovial mood took Aislinn aback. She had never really known the woman to have a lighter side. "Yes…Mother," she said as she slowly got up, looking at the woman askew, trying to figure out this new side of her. Maia gave Aislinn a wink, almost breaking out in a giggle at the sight of Aislinn mentally off-balance.

"Shoo, off with you three!" Maia said, making sweeping gestures with her hands as she pressured them out of her room. She turned around at the doorway, putting a hand to her mouth to keep from laughing, leaving the three of them in the hallway.

Aislinn looked at Farr, who shrugged his shoulders back at her. Damara shook her head at both of them, rolling her eyes. *Either they really are from a different planet, or they are indeed the most foolish people I've ever met to deal with Quia in such a manner,* Damara thought. She tugged at Farr's sleeve, making her way down the hallway toward the stairs. Aislinn watched the pair for a few steps and followed them to the third floor to their respective rooms.

Luigh was on her third lap walking around the city block of the Inn when she all but bounced off Master Glenn's chest.

"Trouble?" He said more than asked.

"If you remain in my way, there will be."

Glenn cocked an eyebrow and studied her face and body language for a moment. Then, he let out a big hearty laugh, moved beside her, and put his arm in hers. Luigh's eyes went wide as she almost had to run to keep up with Glenn or risk getting dragged in the silk dress she was still wearing.

"STOP!" she tried to demand. "Where are you taking me!!!!"

"To blow off some steam." He said with a big toothy grin.

Luigh was so busy holding up her hem and looking where she had to quickly walk that she didn't notice where she was until they stopped. She let her dress go and looked up, breathing hard from the quick walk. A common room as large as the Unicorn's, but not as large, nor opulent, like the one she was staying in. There were some well-dressed men, most likely merchants, but most of the patrons were obvious soldiers from both Parva Frater and Ventus. The air was smokey and loud with laughter. The serving girls had a tough time squeezing around the tables from all the people.

"A bar?!?" Luigh annoyedly said to Glenn.

"Do you gamble?" He amusedly asked, pulling her once again before she could answer.

They zigzagged their way around tables to the far corner.

"Make a hole!" Glenn loudly commanded several times, and the soldiers instinctively moved to let him and Luigh through the throng. Finally, he said it once more at the far corner table, and two soldiers looked up and back to see who was giving commands. Once they realized who it was, they shot up from their seats. Glenn barked out another laugh and slapped them on the shoulders. "Thank you, lads!" He turned to Luigh, "Sit!" saying with a big grin.

Luigh sat and watched as Glenn and five other men, two soldiers from Parva Frater, two soldiers from Ventus, and one well-dressed merchant, took turns shaking a wooden cup. They would slam the cup top down on the table, the person to their left would lift the cup to reveal five dice. Luigh watched this go around the table once, then one of the men, presumably the winner, would collect the pile of coins in the middle of the table. In order to get the cup, one must first pay into the center of the table; the winner of the last round pays first and determines the cost to get the cup of dice.

Luigh watched this go around a few times and figured out it was similar to a game they would play in the barracks on Proximus b called five-card -stud. Although there were no suits in dice, the principle of pairs, straights, flushes, and such seemed the same.

In the third round, Glenn was the previous winner and chose the price to play as one gold Ventus coin. The two guys from Parva Frater smiled and quickly threw-in to match. The two soldiers from Ventus held up their hands, and the turn to pay went to the merchant. He smiled and readily threw down a gold Ventus coin. Glenn was about to start shaking the cup when Luigh threw a gold Occursum coin into the pot. Everyone at the table's eyes widened.

Glenn leaned over at Luigh and said as quietly as he could in the noisy room, "That is way more than the current bet, lass."

"I know," she said, smiling up at him, "I want to play anyway at the current bet. No need to match."

"As you wish, lassie," Glenn said. He looked at the merchant and the two Parva Frater soldiers in a silent question to see if they also agreed. The merchant smiled a sly smile and put nine more gold Ventus coins in the pot. Glenn shook his head and anted up, but the other two soldiers took their Ventus gold back.

Glenn shook the cup and slammed it down on the table. The merchant lifted the cup and announced the dice to the table, "A 4, 3, 5, 2, and another 5."

"Ha! A pair of fives!" Glenn said, smiling.

The merchant scooped up the dice and started shaking as a serving girl handed out big tankards of mead to each of them. He stopped shaking and took a big drink, put it down, and resumed his shaking of the dice. The merchant slammed the cup down, and Luigh lifted it up and announced the dice, "A 6, 6, 6, 2, and a 3." She scooped up the dice and shook them, slammed the cup on the table, and looked up and over at Glenn. He lifted the cup and announced the dice,

"A 2, 3, 6, 4, and a 5! A straight run! The lassie wins!"

Luigh smiled, stood up, and with both hands, swept the coins on the table to be in front of her seat. She took several big swigs of her tankard of mead, wiped her mouth on her sleeve, smiled, and threw 2 gold Ventus coins into the center of the table.

The three of them played several more rounds, with Luigh winning more than she lost. The expression of the merchant's face went from seeing an easy mark, to serious concentration, and finally to disdain.

Luigh had amassed a sizeable pile of gold Ventus coins in front of her. Glenn had stopped playing five rounds ago, "This game is getting too rich for my blood." He guffawed. The merchant had won the last round, and it was his turn to set the ante. He looked at his diminished pile of coins, then askew at Luigh's pile. He let out a barely audible growl and aggressively pushed all of his money into the center of the table. Luigh looked at the pile and squinted, slightly tilting her fully buzzing head.

"How many is that?" she asked Glenn, inebriated too much to count.

Glenn was about to answer when the merchant slammed his palms on the table and slightly stood up, shouting, "FIFTY! NOW PLAY!"

Glenn shot the man a level look. The merchant cleared his throat and slowly sunk back into his seat. Glenn looked down at Luigh and calmly said, "The bet is fifty gold Ventus coins."

Luigh looked at her pile, then the ante pile, then back at hers. Her tongue poked out of her mouth slightly as she thought for a moment, then pushed all of her coins forward, not quite coming close to the center of the table with her short arms.

"You can't do that!" the merchant balked.

Glenn gave the merchant another flat stare, "The lass most certainly can raise the bet, as you have done previously."

The merchant grumbled something under his breath while he rummaged about his person. Finally, he produced a few more gold Ventus coins, some silver Ventus coins, a couple of copper Ventus coins, and a handful of bronze Ventus coins. He studied the lot, sighed, unbelted a long knife, and put that into the pile. "Is that satisfactory to the *lass*?"

Luigh blinked a few times to get the table back into focus, took another swig of her mead, and nodded.

The merchant scoffed as he roughly grabbed the dice cup, shook it so violently he had to put his hand over the opening to keep the dice from flying out, then slammed it down so hard the pile of coins almost scattered across the table.

Luigh stood up, with some stability help from Glenn, and lifted the cup off of the dice. "A, um, 2, 2, 2, 2, and, a, uh, 6."

The merchant laughed as he sat back in his chair, feeling triumphant, "Hah! Four pair!" He stood up and reached out to scoop up what he thought were his winnings.

"Sit!" came the low command from Glenn.

The merchant stopped, stooped over the pile with both arms ready to scoop, and looked at Glenn, surprised.

"It is her turn." Glenn flatly said as he gathered the dice, put them in the cup, and handed it to Luigh.

Luigh smiled up at Glenn and shook the cup, slamming it down on the table.

The merchant's face resigned to a sour as he stopped reaching for the bounty and instead lifted the dice cup off the table to reveal the pips underneath.

His eyes went wide with white, "A 6…6…6…6…6! Immmpppooooosssssiiible!" he hissed. He straightened up fast and pointed a boney finger at Luigh. "*You cheated!*"

Glenn stood up and tensed his muscles, the armor creaking against the strain. "No one cheated. I think it is time for you to leave. Now!"

The merchant looked from Luigh to Glenn, the pile on the table, and back to Glenn.

"PAHH!" he spat as he waved his hand dismissively. "OUT OF MY WAY!" he shouted as he roughly made his way out of the tavern of soldiers.

Luigh looked up at the standing Glenn, "Did we win?"

He looked down at her and smiled, "Aye, lass, you won."

Luigh sat back sloppily, "Sweet! Can you help me carry it back to my room?"

Glenn, still giving her a fatherly smile, "Aye, lass."

He accepted her belt pouch and loaded it to the brim with as many gold coins as he could, then filled his with the rest. He tucked the long knife in his belt, hoisted Luigh up, and helped her walk out of the tavern, "Time to go, lass."

"Aww, already?" Luigh slurred, "ok. Bye, guys!" she waved at the other soldiers around the table. They all laughed, smiled, and waved back at her.

The streets were deserted at this late hour of the night, as Glenn helped keep Luigh on a straight path back to her Inn. He felt a sharp burning in his right shoulder, just below the armored deltoid plating. The arm he had around Luigh went limp as he spun around to face his attacker, drawing his sword with his left arm.

Luigh, not clearly understanding what was going on at the moment, quickly and momentarily sobered up enough to see blood running down Glenn's right arm, and he had his sword out in his left hand. Even more of a puzzle was that he was facing the wrong way from where the Inn was. She turned around to see what he was looking at.

Four armed men, black pants, black shirts, black hooded cloaks, and black coving their mouths, stood on the red brick sidewalk about forty feet from them. Three of the black-clothed men had short swords, and one had a knife in each hand.

Luigh looked down momentarily at their boots, and the man with the knives had brown boots. As time seemed to be moving very slow for her, she grasped at a thought about the man in the brown boots. *I know I just saw them, but where??* Then it hit her, *The tavern, THE MERCHANT!* She looked back up to see Glenn charging the would-be assassins. The merchant quickly stepped to the side and into the empty street to avoid Glenn and let the other three with swords handle him. He set his sights on Luigh and grinned as he threw a knife at her chest.

Luigh saw the knife tumbling at her, handle over blade. She tilted her head at it curiously as it was rapidly heading for her. She reached out with right her hand as if to catch the blade. The knife stopped, the blade tip an inch from her chest and her heart. She looked at the knife, held in mid-air, and cocked her drunk head to the other side, trying to figure it out.

"NO!" the merchant shouted at her in anger, "YOU WERE SUPPOSED TO LEAD ME TO THE BOY OR DIE!"

Luigh looked at the man, *Boy? Rowan? Die?!?* She tried to comprehend. Her face struggled as the understanding came slowly, the fog in her brain clearing with anger.

The merchant threw another knife, and Luigh, now fully aware she was holding Medeis, waved her hand, and both blades flew back and into the merchant. He fell to his knees in the street, a dagger sticking out from each shoulder. Luigh, full of rage, looked at the other three men engaged with Glenn. He was holding his own against all three, with only one good arm, but couldn't do more than give minor cuts and slices here and there: keeping them from gaining any ground on him.

Luigh thought about the three men, their lungs, alveoli, bronchioles, bronchi, and tracheas. She reached out with her hands and made two fists. All three men's eyes popped out of their heads, as all three of their necks and chests caved in, all the air compressed and sucked out. Luigh released her fists, and the three men fell onto the sidewalk in crumpled heaps. Glenn, huffing and puffing, sheathed his sword and walked over to

Luigh. She saw the wound in Glenn's arm and put her hand over it. Still holding Medeis, Luigh easily healed the wound. Glenn shivered and stretched out his right arm, moving it in a small circle.

"Good as new, lass. Thank you." Glenn said, smiling. "The fourth?" he said, motioning to the merchant on his knees in the street, with a knife sticking out of each shoulder, his arms limp and hanging down his sides, tears streaking his cheeks as he whimpered.

"Bring him with us," Luigh told Glenn. "He has information."

"As you wish, Luigh Quia," Glenn said, inclining his head.

Luigh was taken aback by the title Glenn bestowed on her, but she didn't correct him either. Instead, she rubbed her forehead, trying to straighten out her thoughts. *Is there truly nowhere to hide? Will we always be a target? Ugh! That woman! Why does she get to be right?!*

Luigh followed Glenn as he pulled the merchant assassin along to her Inn. Glenn pulled the man up the main stairs. Luigh was thankful the common room was empty as she followed them up to the second floor, dreading that Glenn was going straight to Maia's room.

Glenn paused at the new pine door and looked back at Luigh, who hung her head. He let out a little laugh, "I am safe to assume this is you?" he gestured at the door.

Luigh took a deep breath and looked at Glenn, "She lied to me."

"Quia do not lie. They bend the truth. You have to either learn to read between the lines or pin them down and offer no way out." Glenn lectured her.

"So I am learning," Luigh admitted.

Glenn gave her a knowing nod and knocked on the new door.

"Enter," came the familiar voice from inside the room.

Glenn opened the door with his left hand and drug the merchant in with his right. Luigh stopped short of the door frame in the hallway, took a deep breath, and steeled herself from what she now felt was a well-deserved lecture.

Luigh entered the room and saw the merchant on his knees in the middle of the room, between the living room area and the bedroom area. Glenn still had a good grip on the merchant's left shoulder with his right hand, and Maia stood in front of the defeated man.

Maia looked up and over the merchant when Luigh entered.

"Ah, child. I see you caught us a crow." She said, smiling.

Luigh was confused and not as drunk as she had been since leaving the tavern. *Um, why is she smiling at me? She should be furious with me for how I behaved.*

"Come, let us see what this *shade* knows," Maia said, beckoning Luigh into the room. "Close the door, child."

Luigh closed the door behind her and walked over to Maia's side.

The merchant didn't give up any more information, other than he was to find, follow, and kill anyone matching Luigh's, Aislinn's, or Farr's descriptions. Likewise, he was to find and capture anyone matching Rowan's description. Glenn was more than happy to twist the knives in the man's shoulders to eke out the knowledge.

Resigned to the fact that the merchant would not give up any more knowledge, Maia told Glenn to hand the man over to the King's Guard for attempted murder. Glenn inclined his head and pulled the merchant out of the room, fully intending to dispatch the man out on the street with his other friends.

After Glenn drug the merchant out of the room, Maia closed the door and turned to face Luigh.

Here it comes, Luigh braced herself.

"What do you think now, child?"

"What do you mean?"

Maia cocked an eyebrow at her.

"I mean, child, do you now see that you and your friends are safest with me…even if that means in a battle. I know you feel I lied to you, but I assure you I have not. Aislinn will be most safe next to me, you will be safe in the backfield helping the wounded, and Farr and Damara will be on the far fringes of the battle. I have kept my word to keep you all as safe as I can."

Luigh looked at Maia and exhaled a breath she didn't realize she held, her shoulders dropping. "Yes…mother."

"Good. Now let me help soothe what I'm sure will be a nasty hangover." Maia said as she moved to Luigh and placed her hands on Luigh's head. Luigh shivered and sheepishly smiled at Maia. "Get some rest, child. Stay in the Inn with the others. You will all need it."

"Yes, Mother," Luigh said and made her way out of Maia's room and headed to hers. *Aislinn is* not *going to believe me when I tell her about this!* Luigh laughed at herself.

Only a friend of Oakness may enter
α
δ
γ
ε
ρ
β
τ
φ
υ
ι
η

Chapter 18

A ngus began to disembowel, bleed, skin, and carve up the stag.

"I believe we can risk a small fire for cooking," he told Rowan.

Rowan blinked, then jumped to gathering twigs, brush, and a few medium-sized branches for a fire. He dug out his flint and steel from his pack and began to get the fire going. After a few dozen scraps of the steel on the flint, Rowan successfully got enough of a spark to ignite the detritus and smaller twigs and had a fire going in no time. Angus came over to the fire and nodded approvingly.

He handed Rowan a couple of sharpened sticks, "Here, come stab some meat on them and angle them over the fire."

Rowan sat, watching the meat cook on the spickets over the fire, while Angus looked at Rowan, studying him. Long moments went by, as Angus would occasionally check the meat and turn them when he thought necessary. Finally, Angus took one of the spickets and handed it to Rowan, then took one for himself and sat across from Rowan, the fire in between them.

Rowan was starving and tore into the venison. Angus watched for a brief minute, waiting, then ate himself. They both ate most of the meat, and Angus wrapped the rest in oiled parchment to store in his pack.

"So," Angus started, bent over and his hands stuffing the meat in his pack, "how long have you known?"

"Known what?"

Angus closed his pack up, sinching the straps tight, stood up, faced Rowan, and arched an eyebrow. Rowan knew that look, the *no-bullshit me* look. Rowan sighed. "Since the 'oasis' in Ventus, before the 'man in black' chased us through the portal. Maia started to explain it to me. I still don't understand, but I got the picture pretty clear that I'm a danger to everyone around me."

Angus stood there stoically, looking at Rowan for a few minutes.

"Well?!" Rowan demanded. "Aren't you going to lecture me? Yell at me? Beat me up or something?!?"

Angus just stood there and put his right hand on his chin, in thought. "…no."

"No, what??"

"No, I'm not going to do any of that. You are correct in your assessment of the situation. You are dangerous to everyone and everything."

"You're not going to force me to go back?"

"No. Either you will choose your path, or one will be chosen for you."

Rowan rolled his eyes. "Not more of this 'prophesy' crap!"

"It is how Maia Quia knew how to find you."

"And you trust *her*?"

"With my life."

Rowan threw up his hands in disbelief. "You are all crazy!"

Angus barked a laugh, "Perhaps. Only time will tell."

"Well, I don't intend…" Rowan was saying when Angus held out a hand to stop him and put a finger to his own mouth.

"…shh," Angus hissed.

Rowan stood there, dumbfounded and a little annoyed at being told to shut up.

<snap>

Rowan's head swung around at the sound of a twig cracking in time to see four Fera leap from the brush. In one fluid motion, he slid his left foot in a small arch behind him, pivoting on his right foot, and drew his sword. He rose his blade with an upward stroke, turned his wrists, and sliced the closest Fera from the right armpit to come out the left side of its neck, black blood spurting. Rowan stepped into the now vacant spot and continued his turn, flicking his wrists again, and brought the blade downward at an angle. This one caught the next Fera in the left shoulder, severing the arm, and Rowan's sword became lodged in its ribcage and spine. Rowan kicked the Fera square in the chest and dislodged his sword. The limbless, gasping Fera crashed backward into a third while the fourth stepped around to leap at Rowan. With its sharp fang teeth bared, the fourth Fera let out a snarl, its bat-nose flaring wide, and its bat ears flattened back against its coarsely haired head. Rowan squared up in a mid-ready guard and swung his sword straight across. It cleaved the head cleanly off the leaping Fera. Rowan heard a guttural growl off to his left and turned to see the third Fera had regained its footing from his dead packmate being kicked into it. It charged, and Rowan thrust his sword directly at its chest, turned the blade, and pulled to the side, disemboweling the creature.

Rowan pulled his sword back and regained a low ready posture while he slowly circled, looking for additional threats.

He saw Angus standing in a cleared circle of black course-haired mass. *He must've killed ten to my four! At the same time!!*

Angus was cleaning the blade of the single sword he had drawn when they both heard the low guttural horn. "This was a scouting party. We are found. Do we die here, Rowan, or run? Choose!"

Rowan looked at the large dangerous man, his muscles tightly coiled springs, ready to unleash a torrent of war. *Me? Choose??* "Run!" Rowan shouted, not fully believing what he was saying.

Angus nodded at him and sheathed his sword. Rowan hastily wiped the Fera blood from his blade onto his pant leg before he sheathed his sword.

"Which way?" Angus asked.

Rowan quickly looked around, heard the low tone guttural horn again, and pointed in the opposite direction, up the mountain. "That way!"

Angus didn't say a word and made for the way Rowan had pointed to, picked up his pack as he bounded over the fire, kicking it with his foot, spreading ash, fire, and smoke as a distraction.

Rowan grabbed his pack, flung it over his shoulder, and followed Mr. Mountain up the actual mountain.

They ran as fast as they dared in the darkness, occasionally stopping to hear the bleating of the pursuing horn. They made out two distinct horns, from two directions below them, calling and answering as they closed in on the campfire, joined together, and started up the mountain.

"They are on our trail. Quickly." Angus gruffly said and continued his fast-paced uphill jog. Rowan followed as best he could for about an hour when he began to gasp for breath in the thinning atmosphere.

"Hold up!" Rowan gasped.

Angus turned around, "We must keep going!"

"There! We can lose them in there!" Rowan pointed to a narrow gap between a rockface.

Angus looked at the gap, nodded at Rowan, and squeezed through it. Rowan followed, and his mouth almost dropped open when he popped out the other side. His head went back, and his eye went wide as he followed the massive trees skyward. *A Woodland?!?*

Angus and Rowan moved faster in the Woodland's natural pathways devoid of roots and rocks, and they quickly reached the center.

"Wait here and catch your breath," Angus told Rowan, and he bolted past the Woodland's central portal arch. He was gone for about five minutes when he reappeared from the way they had just come.

"We are trapped here. The vermin are upon the gap. It looks like we make our final stand here. Be ready!"

Rowan looked at Angus incredulously. *Be ready??* Rowan turned and looked at the archway. He saw the smooth stones had a single symbol on each face of the rock, with a capstone at the top.

Only a Friend of Caitheness may enter? Rowan read in his head. *Those symbols look familiar. I wonder…*Rowan reached out with his hand and touched the marks 'Φριενδ'. The ground hummed with vibration, and a light began to glow in the center of the arch. Swirling colors of purple and blue until the entire archway was consumed, illuminated, and pulsated in time with the hum in the ground.

Angus turned to see what Rowan had done.

"Are you mad?!" he exclaimed.

"You told me to choose. I chose! Let's go!"

Angus shook his head. "You have no idea what you are doing."

They both felt it. On top of the humming of the portal. The fear.

Angus looked back to the trail. Gliding across the ground, an Arbitrium. Angus didn't hesitate. He pushed Rowan through the portal and leaped after him.

Rowan rolled on the dusty ground. Angus almost stood over him, furiously touching the Woodland portal stones. The bright glow in the center of the archway blinked out, and Rowan's eyes were left with the after-flash of the light.

His eyes started to adjust to the sudden loss of light, helped by the torch Angus somehow produced and managed to get lit. Rowan pushed himself up off the gritty, dusty stonelike ground, littered with tiny pebbles. He dusted himself off and looked around. He couldn't see anything beyond the edge of the torchlight, just endless blackness.

"Where are we?" Rowan asked in wonder. He noticed that his voice sounded like it drifted into and along the blackness, almost like an echo.

"We are on the Path," Angus said as if Rowan should know.

"Ah, I see." Rowan sarcastically responded.

Angus looked at him flatly, "This may be more dangerous than what we had just left."

"Ohhh? How exactly?" Rowan breathed, confused.

"Follow me closely. Stay in the middle of the Path or fall forever."

"Fall? Forever??" Rowan asked.

Angus ignored the questions and started walking. Rowan had to take a few quick steps to catch up. *Out of the microwave, and into the ion blast,* he thought. They walked for what felt like a mile to Rowan and came to what looked like a large stone fountain, long since dry. Only dust and more pebbles where water should have pooled. Angus held the torch up to see the fountain better. Rowan walked around the perimeter.

"This feels like an island."

"It is. In a way. More of a waypoint on the Path." Angus said, studying what looked like a map carved into the top of the stone that would've surrounded the fountain pool. It was severely pitted, reminding Rowan of the Obelisk on that strange hot other dimension world with the bear creatures.

<Harrrrrooooooon> came the low tonal bleat of a horn.

"Blast. It knows how to work the Portal. This way, quickly!" Angus said, running around the fountain to another pathway leading away. The Path felt like it arched upward to Rowan for about two miles before it leveled off, and they came to another dead fountain. Angus looked for the carved map and attempted to decipher another pitted version.

<Harrrooon. Harrooon.>

"Damn. It's driving them in after us." Angus said. "This way!" He pointed and quickly took off down another Path. They jogged for about a half-mile when Angus had stopped short, causing Rowan to almost run into his back.

"What gives?" Rowan asked.

"The Path is gone." Angus pointed out with the torch. Rowan looked around the big guy and saw the Path was broken, leading to nothingness.

"Quickly, back to the fountain!" Angus commanded, and they ran back to the second fountain. Angus ran a quarter of the way around it and down another Path. This one felt like it went down in a spiral for a mile before it also leveled off and led to another fountain. Angus quickly located another badly damaged map.

<Harrrooon>

"This way!" and he took off down a Path. They ran for about two miles in a slow arch to what felt like Rowan's right.

<Harrroon>

The bleating of the horn was getting closer, and at the next fountain, Angus didn't have any time to find the map. He threw his torch into the empty fountain pool and drew his sword.

"SIDE BY SIDE!" he shouted, taking a defensive stance with the Path attached to the fountain island. Rowan unsheathed his sword and took up a low ready posture on Angus' right.

<Haroon>

Rowan saw the tapetum lucidum of the Fera flashing in the darkness and heard their guttural growls and snarls as they ran towards Angus and him.

All the training, hours, and pain he had endured with Angus had not only served to help him become competent with the sword but also helped Rowan to know how the man fought, where he might bring his blade next. In this narrow fatal funnel, it allowed the two, not only to hold twenty Fera at bay, but completely decimate them like a woodchipper. It was over in less than two minutes, and Angus wasn't even breathing hard. *What the hell? How does he do that??* Rowan thought as he gained control of his own rapid breathing.

Angus went over to the fountain, picked up the still-burning torch, and located the crumbling map. He was tracing his fingers on the map when…

<Harrrooooon>

"You've got to be kidding me!" Rowan said exasperatedly.

"I estimate thirty more Fera for the one Arbitrium. More if there is another Arbitrium or even a Beluinus. We need to get out of here. This way!" Angus said as he went to the other side of the fountain and took off down the Path at a dead run. It was all Rowan could do to keep up with him for the first three miles, at a slight downhill.

Rowan felt the torchlight begin to pull away, and darkness started to creep in around him.

"HEY!" Rowan shouted at Angus, "Hold up!"

Angus slowed to a fast jog to allow Rowan to catch up but not stop.

Two more miles and they came to another fountain. Angus found the map and the following Path quickly. Rowan barely had time to catch his breath when the big man bounded up the following Path. Angus didn't go at a full run but kept up a fast pace. Rowan felt like this Path went uphill and slightly to the right. They were on this part of the Path for only two miles before it leveled off at yet another fountain.

"This place is a maze!!" Rowan declared.

"Even more so now," Angus admitted as he searched for the carved map.

<Harrrroooon>

"They just don't know when to quit, do they?" Rowan asked.

"They never do." Angus replied flatly, "This way!"

Angus went a quarter of the way around the left side of the fountain and found the next part of the Path. He went down it at a quick jog, with Rowan closely following.

They didn't have long to go before they came to the familiar stones of the Woodland archway. Angus touched the stones in the same pattern Rowan had previously done 'Φριενδ' and the portal sprung to life.

"Quickly now!" Angus commanded as he threw the torch over the side of the Path. Rowan watched as the light from the torch faded, being swallowed up by the darkness. He felt hands grab him and throw him through the portal.

Rowan slammed into a large wooden crate and got the wind knocked out of him, and his vision doubled. When he could see straight, he saw Angus press the same symbols on this side of the portal, and it winked out. There was a slight depression behind the archway that became a stone wall.

"Where are we?" Rowan asked.

"It appears to be a cellar," Angus said dryly.

"No shit, Sherlock." Rowan retorted. "I meant where on *Earth* are we?!"

"That, I am not entirely sure. I've never used the Path before. Who is…*Sherlock?*"

"What?? NEVER?!" Rowan said, shocked, ignoring Angus' missed literary reference.

"It is forbidden." Angus maintained his dry demeanor. "Try to stay quiet and let us venture up and out to see where we are."

Rowan nodded and followed Angus around the maze of large boxes. The air was musty and thick. Any dust they stirred up seemed to hang suspended in the stale air. Rowan saw that most of the crates had the word 'Fairharbour' burned on them. He thought that it might be the name of the establishment they had broken into.

Angus found some wooden stairs that led up to an angled double doorway. He pressed his ear to the door for a moment, then slowly pushed the doors upward. They moved about a quarter of an inch, then the distinct sound of a chain being brought taught sounded. "Locked." Angus hissed. He motioned for Rowan to take a few steps back down, unsheathed his sword, put the point in the center of where both doors met and twisted. A loud snap of metal, then the clanging of the chain falling on the other side of the door could be heard, making Rowan wince for fear of being discovered. Angus pushed against the doors gently again. This time they opened to reveal it was nighttime outside. Angus exited first and waved Rowan up.

"Welcome to Ab Oriente. More specifically, Hangetsu Minato." Angus said as Rowan stepped out of the cellar and into the alleyway.

Rowan could smell the salt air and felt the humidity hit him like a wet towel, almost breaking out in a sweat. He looked up at the night sky.

"Wait, shouldn't it be daytime by now?"

"Time and distance move differently on the Path. We are clear across the continent. Far South of Baile Atha Cliath."

"Nooooo!" Rowan said, not believing. "That is thousands of kilometers, I, uh, mean miles!"

"Aye, hundreds of leagues in a matter of hours on the Path, but almost instantaneous in the real world."

"This place kills me," Rowan said, shaking his head.

"It may yet," Angus said, not getting the sarcasm. "We must find an Inn. Stay close. The people here are not as, shall we say, friendly towards outsiders."

"Oh, that's a surprise, this planet gets better and better." Rowan laughed.

Angus cocked an eyebrow, getting that sarcasm, and grunted. "Come."

Chapter 19

Maia bolted up in her bed. The Vinculum pounding in her head. Angus was being attacked by Viventem but quickly dispatched them. She wiped the sweat-soaked hair from her forehead and looked out one of the windows near her bed. *Still the middle of the night.* She weaved a tiny thread of Fire and lit a taper candle on her nightstand. As she began to get up, she fell back onto the bed, shuddered again by the Vinculum, this time an overwhelming sense of urgency. *They are being pursued!*

Maia pushed through the feelings and got up off the bed, splashed cool water on her face, and changed her sweaty small clothes. Sitting back down on the bed, she took a deep breath and slowly let it out, centering herself. Reaching out through the Vinculum, she attempted to bring calm to it, adding her strength to Angus'. She sat there, in a meditative state for a couple of hours. Maia's meditation popped like a bubble, and she sat up ridged, her eyes popping wide open in shock.

The Fear.

The Dread.

An Arbitrium.

No! They are surrounded!! Maia felt the strain in her forearms; she had been clenching her fists and pulling on her bedspread. She let go of the bedding and took another deep breath. *He will need all my strength to defeat it without me there to distract it.* Another cleansing breath, she closed her eyes and felt along the Vinculum sending calming strength.

Suddenly, nothing!

Again, Maia's eyes went wide, this time in surprise, as she shot to her feet. *He's not dead. He can't be! I would have felt that!! Did Rowan find another Obelisk??* Maia smoothed out her long shift clothing, closed her eyes, took a couple of cleansing breaths to relax, and reached out along the Vinculum. She felt the tendrils that connected her to Angus flow out like a ribbon, though the wall of the Inn, northwest, out of the Ventus Capital, in an undulating straight line into the Northern Mountains, until it abruptly stopped, as if cleanly cut with a pair of shears. *That's not possible. An Arbitrium cannot just sever the link! It only knows to kill. The Vinculum would have snapped back at me. It is still connected, but to where?!?* Maia opened her eyes, perplexed at what might have occurred. She reflexively smoothed out her shift again in the single dim candlelight. She pulled on one of her purple riding dresses and decided to go downstairs to get something stronger than water to drink to help calm her nerves.

Maia made her way down the main stairs to the common room from the third floor without seeing anyone. She walked behind the bar and filled a tankard with ale from a tapped keg. Making her way around the bar to a table to sit down, came a familiar voice from across the room.

"Trouble sleeping, Maia Quia?"

Maia strained her eyes in the dimly lit room, saw the amber glow of a pipe, and she strode over to it; the shadowy figure came into clearer view.

"I could ask the same of you, Maighstir Glenn." She said coolly as she sat down.

"Ah, well, it was my turn on watch."

"I didn't know we were in peril here?"

"Well, after the *merchant*, the Leifteanant and I thought it would be best. Besides, we will need to get back to keeping watches later tonight."

"Hmm, prudent. Later tonight? Do you know the time?"

"Why yes, Maia Quia, it is one in the morning."

"Ah, thank you, Maighstir Glenn."

"You still haven't said what is obviously troubling you. Certainly not the battle. We have formulated a solid plan as any." Glenn narrowed his eyes at Maia, attempting to unravel an enigma, "Is it Angus? Have you word??"

Maia smiled motherly at Glenn. Even though Glenn looked like he could be Maia's father, Maia has known Glenn since he was a child. Such is one benefit of the connection with Medeis; the stronger the connection, the longer the life.

"You have always been very perceptive, Maighstir Glenn. It is Angus, and no, I have not received word from him. It appears that…"

Maia's eyes went wide, her body stiff, then she fell off her chair as if knocked to the side or whipped around in a semicircle. Glenn shot up and rushed to her side to help her up.

"Maia Quia!"

"I am…alright." She breathed, holding her head in her hands. When the shock wore off and her dizzy feeling subsided, she looked up at Glenn standing over her with a proffered hand. She took it, and he pulled her to her feet.

"What happened??"

"It appears I do have word from Angus…and he is in Ab Oriente."

"Ab Oriente?? How?!?"

"Of that, Maighstir Glenn, I do not know. But I intend to find out."

Maia picked up her tankard from the table and took a long pull from it. "Thank you for your company, Maighstir Glenn. I will see you in a few hours."

"Sleep well, Maia Quia." He said as he held his fist to his upper left chest in a salute. Maia inclined her head in return and walked back to the bar, placing the half-drunk tankard on the polished and well-oiled maple bar.

She glanced back at the shadowy figure of Glenn and saw the amber glow of his pipe bowl resume its light from a seated position. Maia smiled to herself, *He has always been a perceptive boy, well, man now. I can only hope he will be just as keen in the days to come.* She let her smile slowly fade in her thought of Master Glenn as she made her way back to her room. Sleep came quickly, as she was emotionally exhausted from the last couple of hours and a night of very interrupted sleep.

Maia's second sleep was longer than her first, but not long enough for her liking, as she felt rudely awoken to a banging at her new door.

"Yes?" she managed to croak out of her sleepy throat.

"Maia Quia. It has been thirty minutes past the time you told us to meet you downstairs." came the familiar female voice.

"I'll be down in fifteen minutes, Aislinn. Make sure you are all packed and ready to ride by then."

"Yes, Mother." came the expected reply.

Good. I will need that one to respond immediately and expediently in the next few days if this is to work. Maia stretched her arms and legs out easily in the large king-sized bed for a person of her stature. She rubbed the sleep from her eyes, swung her legs over the side, and stood up, slightly stretching again. She washed up with the bone-white porcelain basin and matching pitcher. Maia didn't need to change her small clothes, as she felt they were clean after she had changed in the middle of the night. She put on the same riding dress she went down in very early in the morning. Maia quickly packed up her belongings, a three-day change of clothes, some jewelelry, tied her belt purse to her simple dark leather belt, and took a last look around the room to make sure she got everything.

Satisfied everything was packed in less than five minutes, she left her room and made her way down to the common room, knowing she had enough time to still eat breakfast before they had to leave and meet up with the men from Parva Frater.

Aislinn quickly made her way down to the common room after Maia had given her instructions. Breathing rapidly upon reaching the table where Farr, Damara, and Luigh were still eating breakfast, "Mother, um, I mean…Maia wants us to be packed and down here in fifteen minutes."

Luigh snickered, "Do you hear yourself?? *Mother wants?* Really Ais, get a grip."

"Well, we're stuck here, like it or not, Luigh, and I'm going to do what I need to figure this all out. You can be as obstinate as a bulkhead for all I care."

Luigh's eyes widened at the blatant insubordination she would expect from Rowan, but not Aislinn. Luigh's eyes narrowed, and her mouth tightened as she placed both of her hands down on the table and pushed herself up to look across the table at Aislinn.

"Ensign," Luigh softly hissed, "you forget to whom you are speaking."

Aislinn's face flushed with embarrassment, but she planted her hands firmly on her hips and returned the stare.

"I do not, *Captain*. It is *you* who forgets where we *are!*"

Luigh's eyes widened in hurt and shock as she sunk down in her chair, deflated. She hid her face in her hands as silent sobs racked her body and shook her shoulders.

"That was a bit uncalled for, Aislinn," Farr said as he got up and walked around the table to comfort Luigh.

"But…she said…oh, I give up!" Aislinn said as she fell into an empty chair at the table.

Farr soothed Luigh by gently rubbing her back, "It has been hard and confusing for all of us. Of course, it is not your fault, but we must do things we would normally not have to, to survive here. We must break our molds and remake ourselves."

Luigh sniffled and picked up a napkin to blow her nose. She wiped her face with both sleeves, looked at Farr, and smiled, lightly patting him on his diminutive shoulder.

"Ais, I'm sorry," Luigh said, stretching out her hand to Aislinn.

Aislinn saw Luigh reach out, slightly shocked with the apology but hearing it more often lately than all the years she has known her. Aislinn grew up in the same sector of Proximus b, and looked up to Luigh for as long as she could recall. Aislinn slowly reached out and took

Luigh's hand, and they grasped each other and smiled, both welling up with tears.

Luigh collected herself first and gave Aislinn's hand a squeeze before letting it go. "Farr is right. We must remake ourselves here. If you want to immerse yourself with the Quia, I'm not going to stand in your way. I, however, will remain myself." Luigh took a deep breath and let it out, "but, I will go with you and learn from them." Luigh looked from Aislinn to Farr and smiled at Damara, "I will always try to keep my crew safe."

"Well, I guess that means we should get packing," Farr said with a smile.

Luigh let out a surprised laugh, "On to the next adventure!"

Aislinn clapped her hands together in glee, but Damara looked at the three with concern. *They don't know battle, let alone war.* The young Damara, by Caitheness standards, remembered what she had read, the firsthand account of stories she had heard, and the hiding she had gone through when it had once threatened her Woodland. *How many will die in the next few days?* She looked at Farr, *I will die before anything hurts you!*

Farr tugged at Damara's sleeve, "Love? Are you coming??"

Damara blinked, even though she was looking at him, she didn't realize Farr had come back around the table to her. "Ah, yes, mo chridhe." She pushed herself away from the table, and the two lovers followed Luigh and Aislinn to go pack for their next 'adventure'.

Chapter 20

Maia was with Master Glenn at one of the tables when Luigh, Aislinn, Farr, and Damara came down into the common room, full packs on each of their backs and dressed for travel. When they reached the table, Maia was just finishing her tea and delicately wiped the corners of her lips.

"…not a problem. Adjustments should be easy with our formation." Glenn was saying as the group walked up to the table. Glenn saw them approach, "Ah, good. Shall we?" he said to them as he got up from the table, holding Maia's pack.

Maia placed the napkin down on the table with a few gold Occursum coins and got up from the table.

"Good, children. I hope you all had a good rest and a hearty breakfast." She said as she examined each one of them in turn. "We will be eating and sleeping rougher for the next few days."

"We have, Mother," Aislinn said, beaming at Maia. Luigh bit her lip.

"Good…good. Time to go, children. I will go over the plan once we are on the road."

They followed Glenn out of the back of the Inn to the stables in the alleyway. Their horses were all saddled and waiting. Two stable boys each holding a horse, and a third holding the reins of two horses. Glenn went and took a rein from the third stable boy and helped Maia up on the horse. The other three stable boys helped Aislinn, Farr, and Damara on their horses. Luigh stood there for a moment, realizing there wasn't a horse for her.

"What gives?" Luigh said with her hands on her hips.

"I thought you didn't want help with your horse?" Glenn shot back with a sly smile.

Aislinn, Farr, Damara, and even Maia hid chuckles of laughter, remembering the last time Glenn tried to help Luigh on her horse.

"Fine!" Luigh said as she stomped into the stable.

Glenn waited for a couple of minutes when Maia prompted him to go after Luigh.

Glenn entered the stable to see Luigh struggling to lift the saddle and place it on her horse's back.

"The blanket needs to go on first, Mistress Luigh."

Luigh gave a resigned loud sigh, took the caddy-corner saddle off the horse's back, and placed it on the ground.

"Will you show me?"

"It would be my pleasure, Mistress Luigh."

"Please, just 'Luigh'."

"As you wish…Luigh." Glenn said with a wink.

He walked over to the side of a stall and took the blanket striped in dark shades of grey that was hanging over it. He folded it and placed it evenly over the horse's back. Next, he picked up the saddle and placed it in the middle of the blanket on top of the horse.

"See the large belt?"

Luigh nodded.

"Carefully reach under and pull one side to the other."

Luigh bent down next to the horse and reached under. She was almost entirely under the belly of the horse and grabbed the non-buckle end of the belt. She pulled it under and up as she stood back up.

"Good. Now, it's like any other belt. Just feed it through, pull it snug and tight, and secure it."

Luigh followed his directions, and the horse barely moved, used to this maneuver.

"Now, tuck the loose end in the loop, untie the reins and hold them in your left hand as you put your left foot in the stirrup."

Luigh did as directed, giving the horse a soothing pat as it sniffed her while she untied the reins from a post on the outside of the stall.

"Now, hop up, swinging your free leg up and over while using your left hand to grab the pommel and pull. You may need to grab the opposite side of the saddle with your right hand to help pull you up."

Glenn moved a little closer to Luigh in case she needed a little boost in height.

Luigh, with her left foot in the stirrup, holding the reigns and the pommel in her left hand, her right hand hooked on the far side of the saddle, crouched down a little and pushed off her right foot while she pulled with her hands. She just barely gained enough altitude to swing her right leg over the back of the saddle and landed in the saddle. She looked down at Glenn and smiled.

"Well done, lass!" He said, beaming up at her like a father.

"You're an excellent teacher!" She beamed back praise like a daughter.

"Time to go…Luigh." Glenn said, switching his tone to a more somber note.

Luigh nodded at him and led her horse out of the stable to the others waiting in the alleyway, with Glenn following on foot.

The group followed Glenn down the alleyway and out to the street, where the whole host from Parva Frater was waiting near the front of the Inn. The dark purple-blue glow of the early morning was giving way to a deeper blue as Glenn took his reins from one of the other soldiers and mounted his horse. Maia led the group up to the front of the regiment to where Lieutenant MacGill was with his bannerman. Glenn also rode up to the other side of MacGill. The men gave each other nods, and Glenn shouted back at the regiment, "AIR ADHART!"

The command was repeated down the right-hand side, and the host began to move forward at an easy canter down the street and to the southern gate of Mächtige Mauer.

They met with the regiment from Ventus at the southern gate, Maia, Glenn, and MacGill exchanging salutations and greetings with Grüber, Müller, and Bracke. The combined army rode south like a slow caterpillar on the road that was now called the 'Fairharbour Way'.

They rode for a full day and made camp on the large flat prairie plain. Both regiments set up tents for themselves and picket lines for the horses. MacGill had two tents set up for Maia's group near his and Glenn's.

The tents were arranged in groups of ten that faced a central campfire. MacGill led the group to their circle and pointed out their two tents to Maia.

"Aislinn, Luigh, and I will take that one," she pointed, "Farr, you and Damara can have the other."

"Good. I will have dinner brought to you as soon as it's ready." MacGill told Maia, giving her a salute, and he and Glenn strode off to where the wagons were parked.

"Come, children, let us put our packs away and rest until dinner arrives."

Aislinn and Luigh followed Maia into their assigned tent, while Farr and Damara went into theirs. The slate grey canvas tent was spartan, having only three canvas cots that seemed to be made from the leftover cloth of the tents and a center pole made from pine that had an unlit oil lamp hanging from it. Aislinn and Luigh, having spent many a night on the ground, welcomed the cots but missed a proper bed.

Maia placed her pack under one of the cots along the backside of the tent and laid down upon it. Aislinn and Luigh took a cot against each side of the tent, having to duck slightly as the sides were angled from floor to roof.

"Mother?" Aislinn asked.

"Yes, child," Maia answered with her eyes closed and her hands resting on her flat stomach.

"Are you going to go over the plan?"

"At dinner, when we are all together. I do not want to repeat myself. Now get some rest, child."

"Yes, Mother."

They didn't rest long enough to sleep, but it felt good to Luigh and Aislinn to not feel the plodding of a horse beneath them. Finally, a soldier called from outside the main flap of the tent, "Maia Quia, dinner is ready."

Maia opened her eyes and got up from the cot. "Thank you. We will be out momentarily. Please inform Master Farr and Mistress Damara."

"As you wish, Maia Quia."

They heard the soldier's footsteps walk a few yards away, and he called out and informed Farr and Damara of the meal.

"Who's hungry?" Maia asked.

"I'm starved, Mother!" Aislinn said with a big grin as she stood up and rubbed her belly.

"Let's go, children."

They all met near the campfire, where they saw a serving table set up and another table that could seat ten people. Farr examined the tables and was astonished how they could obviously be folded and taken apart for transport.

Maia began to serve herself buffet style, and the group followed her lead, taking seats at the table when they had full plates. There were ten pewter mugs and a large pewter pitcher in the center of the table, and Maia filled five mugs with the water that the pitcher held. Then, she passed out the cups, taking the last one for herself. They started to eat when MacGill and Glenn walked over from a circle of tents nearby. They served themselves and joined the group at the table.

"The men of Ventus are still in agreement, Maia Quia," MacGill said after swallowing a spoonful of stew.

"Excellent. Thank you, Leifteanant MacGill." She then addressed the group. "Children, in case you have forgotten, Farr and Damara will act as left-wing scouts. They will *not* engage unless in defense of their life. They will only report if there are any surprises different than what we expect the Meridiem tactic will be. Luigh, you will be with the rear guard helping with any wounded that will arrive. Use your knowledge with Medeis. Aislinn, you will be with me. I will Join with you and draw on your Medeis to aid mine…"

"Wait, what? Join Medeis?!?" Luigh interrupted.

Maia let out a small sigh, "Yes, child. If one Quia surrenders control to another, they can Join their collective Medeis. That is how a Conclave works."

"Wait, a Conclave?"

"I thought I covered that in Das Daingneach?"

"Glossed over is more like…Mother"

"Ah, well, I shall repeat, and hopefully, you will grasp it this time. A Conclave is made up of twelve joined Quia. We do not know why, but twelve is the maximum strength that can be achieved. The Joining deteriorates rapidly if more than twelve are tried." Maia looked at Aislinn, "It is imperative that you heed me the whole time we are Joined."

Aislinn swallowed hard, "Yes…Mother."

Luigh gave Aislinn a worried look, and Aislinn held her hand halfway up off the table to forestall her. Luigh grimaced but held her tongue.

Maia continued, "The regiment of Parva Frater will look and act like the main host, while the regiment from Ventus will try and attack laterally. We must and will hold our ground until the Conclave from Occursum arrives."

"So, we are a decoy??" Luigh spat disgustedly.

Maia raised an eyebrow at her.

"…mother."

"Yes, that is why you will be needed with any wounded. Your knowledge and ability with Medeis will be most needed."

"Wait," interjected Aislinn, "I thought Quia can't do harm to people?"

Maia turned to Aislinn, "True, but there is no rule against self-defense, human or otherwise."

"HAH!" Luigh blurted out. "So, if you put yourself in the middle of a battle, you are free to do as you please!"

"I told you months ago. The Servire Et Tueri is an Oath all Quia take, but we have learned to bend it over the millennia. As you have pointed out, the first one is by putting oneself in a certain position; the second has never been bent since the War of Power, the third, well, truth is subjective. So, always read between the lines. As for the last and my promise to you, Luigh, I have and will continue to do my best to keep you all safe…as long as you heed me. So, in that, you do not need to question as fact."

"Ok, *mother.* I will follow this 'plan' of yours but mark *my* words; *I will also not let harm come to my crew.*" Luigh said flatly with particular animosity to Maia.

Aislinn, Farr, and Damara all watched and listened, each stuck in various states of eating, afraid to raise a spoon, chew what's in their mouth, or swallow as they watched two cats circle each other while they hissed warnings.

"I would expect nothing less from you, child," Maia said coolly, taking a spoonful of stew.

"Good. We finally agree." Luigh said, also resuming her meal.

Seeing that the two felines set their territories and relaxed, the others also relaxed and thawed from their frozen actions.

They finished their meal with MacGill and Glenn giving Maia reports on troop readiness and expectations. If the Meridiem army approaches in this formation, then they will adjust to this formation, and so on. They broke from dinner with MacGill and Glenn getting up first, saying their goodnights to the group. The group, engrossed in the dinner conversation, hadn't noticed the campfires and torches were lit to aid in travel from one group of tents to the next. The sun had set entirely, and the sky was transitioning from a deep purple to black perforated with glimmering white specks like tiny diamonds.

"We should get our rest. We have one more full day of riding before we get to the plain we picked out to meet the Meridiem army. Come Aislinn, we need to work on Joining."

"Yes, Mother," Aislinn said, getting up from the table.

Luigh said goodnight to Farr and Damara and followed the other women. She wanted to see how Joining was done, even though she had no intention of ever giving up control to another – especially with Medeis.

Maia and Aislinn practiced for about three hours until Maia was satisfied that Aislinn could surrender control fast enough. Luigh watched and learned as she saw the glow of Medeis spring up from Maia first, then Aislinn. Maia wove threads of Air, Water, Fire, and Earth and cast them about Aislinn. When Maia pulled on the weave, Maia instructed Aislinn to will her Medeis to Maia. Luigh saw Aislinn's glow extend to Maia's. Maia would break the threads, and the Medeis would separate back to the respective person. Maia explained to Aislinn that she too can break the Joining at any time, but it would be inadvisable during the battle, as it would cause Maia to lose her concentration, and her weaves could have dire consequences.

After the lesson, they all went to sleep in their cots, the soft glow from the oil lamp on the post snuffed out by Maia. They were woken just before daybreak by another Parva Frater soldier that breakfast was ready. Luigh, Aislinn, and even Maia got up slowly, all three far too used to the cozy beds from the Mächtige Mauer Inn, then a cot out on the plains. Luigh audibly missed her bed more than the other two women as she groaned while she stretched.

They ate breakfast without MacGill and Glenn, Maia explaining that they had already eaten and were making preparations to break camp and get the regiment moving as soon as possible. The group ate quickly, with the conversation dominantly on how much Luigh missed the beds at the Inn.

They didn't have much in the way of facilities, only quick tents set up as makeshift outhouses, which Farr had to stand guard to allow the women to use in private. They were ready to go as soon as they concluded their business and grabbed their packs from the tents. Glenn and two other soldiers brought the group's horses to them as other soldiers quickly disassembled the camp. The group mounted and followed Glenn to the road where MacGill waited with his bannerman. They didn't have to wait long for the regiment to gather in their formation on the road. The soldiers were very efficient and had a lot of training in much harsher climates and terrain than here in Ventus. Glenn gave the command from MacGill for the regiment to move, and the slow caterpillar bristling with swords began to move South.

Maia was correct that it would be a full day of riding until they properly stopped for the night at the top of a small hill. The regiment from Parva Frater lost one wagon to a wheel braking, and the Ventus regiment lost three wagons. Glenn was obviously concerned at dinner that those supplies would be late in arriving at the camp before morning.

"Maia Quia, with all due respect, this endeavor is very well calculated, and everything is accountable as being vital for our success."

"Ture, Maighstir Glenn, but they will be here in a few hours. Your men know what they are about. Trust in them; you have trained them well."

"Acht. That may as well be, Maia Quia." Glenn said with a dismissive hand, embarrassed by the compliment.

They ate the rest of their dinner with an ominous pall falling over the entire camp. The horses whinnied every once and a while. The sounds of eating could clearly be heard above the silence of little to no conversation on the eve of battle.

"Get rest, children. Tomorrow, we face the enemy."

All four of them felt a shiver run through them.

"Yes, Mother." All four found themselves saying in unison.

Chapter 21

Vermi opened his mouth wide, looking like a snake trying to unhinge his jaw. He didn't even try and hide it or stifle it. They had been doing the slash and burn march North for over a month.

"No. No. No. You don't pull it in. You push it back."

"Ohhh. So, I don't want it?" Joesiph furrowed his brow and raked a hand through his hair.

"No. Ugh. How can I explain?" Vermi scratched his goatee.

"It's a dance."

"Dance??"

"More like a death dance," Juventus murmured.

Vermi's head swung around at the comment and arched a suspicious eye at Kaylee Quia. He stroked his goatee and squinted at her. It was not the first utterance that caught his attention.

"Yes, more like a *death* dance. It's a give and take. A push and pull. A very thin balance. Like splitting a hair on a blade over a fire."

"I don't know. I feel like I'm just going to burn up."

"Yes. Exactly." Vermi nodded at the young man in his simple farmer clothing.

"Now, try again. This time, reach out and unravel a yarn-sized tendril of Earth and Air. Intertwine it around that lone tree over there." Vermi pointed.

Joesiph's blond hair became matted to his forehead and moved with his upper eyelashes as he blinked, and beads of sweat trickled down his scruffy cheeks.

Joesiph reached out with his hands, and the thin short poplar tree shook its final brown leaves free. The tree vibrated with increasing intensity, then exploded with a loud crack like thunder in a cloudless sky.

Joesiph let out a breath and wiped his brow with the back of his sleeve. The horses didn't jump. They were battle-trained and getting used to the sudden explosions over the past month.

"Good. Now, the next time, use Fire and Air in the same manner on people."

"Wait! What?? No one said anything about people!"

"Oh, dear boy." Juventus crooned, "What do you think you have been doing this whole time?"

"Well, I, um, thought we were just clearing land for Meridiem to farm."

"No. You are fighting for your life. You heard it for yourself. The Quia I warned you about, killed your parents."

Joesiph looked over his shoulder at the woman, bound, bruised, torn, defeated, and led by a thick rope tied to Kaylee's horse. He looked back at Kaylee with narrowed eyes, a burning fire of hatred in them.

"Good," Juventus said to Joesiph, then turned to Vermi, "Lord Vermi, we should meet the opposition in the next day or so."

"Oh? And how exactly do you know that??"

"I have my sources. The army of Ventus has joined with a force from Parva Frater and a Conclave from Occursum not far behind."

Vermi looked askew at Kaylee. *This woman knows more than she should. Who is she…really?*

Juventus smiled back at Vermi as his mind scrambled for an angle.

"I believe we will ride past a nice knoll that overlooks a wide plain, surrounded by some high brush that could hide a flanking maneuver. We could camp on that knoll and make our final plan?"

Vermi scratched at his goatee.

"What do you think?"

Vermi tilted his head from one side to the next. He was not the most brilliant tactician; that was Aries. But he followed that man into hell itself and learned a little.

"I agree. Are you sure our prisoner doesn't know anything else?"

"I assure you, she does not."

"Then why keep her?"

"She amuses me." Juventus smiled and looked back at the woman. *At least Bella Quia's sobs are only at night now. Should I tell Vermi about the Quia with the Parva Frater force? Hmm, no. He would run; that's always been his style. This may give me the opportunity to kill two birds with one stone.*

Vermi studied Kaylee's expressions of joy and little empathy for the broken woman. *Maybe she really is just one of these feeble 'Quia' the way she protects that woman. I still don't trust her though.*

Vermi turned his attention to the two Meridiem captains.

"Pass the word. We make camp on the next rise."

"As you command, my Lord."

Vermi sat up in his saddle, straining to appear taller than he clearly was. Juventus caught it out of the corner of her eye. *Still the same old Vermi,* she chuckled to herself.

They made camp on top of the knoll Juventus had suggested, just as the hot ball of sun began to set behind the Western Mountains. They had a good vantage of the plain, ringed by miles of thick, tall sagebrush and a few poplar trees jutting out above like islands in a sea of brown.

Juventus ensured that Gildred, Hamala, and Junis slept in the bleached white cotton tent next to hers. She, of course, had a tent to herself. Juventus mused that the 'ants' must be grateful for the white of the tents in this heat, though with her tricks, it never touched her. It was near midnight, by the announcing and changing of guard watch, that she had been waiting for. Juventus left her tent, the dried yellow grass softly crunching under her shoes like straw. Making her way to where Bella was tied up near the horses, like one of the animals.

"…ohhh, you poor thing. Here, have some water."

Bella, on her knees, hands bound tight with a rope tied to the picket line between two horses, lifted her dirty head, scuff marks on her cheeks, chin, and forehead, and her once straight mousey-brown hair a rat's nest filled with dried grass and dirt. Juventus' nose wrinkled at the smell of her, worse than the horses. Bella took the offered waterskin and gulped down the contents, the water splashing all over her face and making streaks in the dirt on her cheeks.

"Easy, girl. Easy. You don't want a cramp."

Bella finished the waterskin and slowly tried to wipe her mouth on what was left of her sleeve.

"Why…why are you being nice?"

"Why, girl. You wound me. I've always been nice to you." Juventus smiled evilly.

Bella recoiled from the smile, dropping the waterskin, and backed away from Juventus until the rope to the picket line was taught.

"Oh, girl. Do not be afraid. I am here to release you."

"Release…me? Why? Why now?"

"You will deliver a message for me."

Juventus' smile deepened as she made the weaves for Coacta. She undid Bella's bindings and helped her onto a horse.

"Do you understand, girl?"

"Yes, mistress."

"Good. Now go."

Bella rode the horse at full gallop eastward. Juventus watched her go for a few moments, then made her way back to her tent, humming a long-forgotten tune.

Later in the early morning, she was awoken to shouts and scrambling outside her tent. She poked her head out of the front flap, shielding her eyes from the red morning glow.

"You there!" she pointed at a Meridiem guard. "What is all the fuss about?"

"The prisoner has escaped, Kaylee Quia."

"Oh my! My sisters and I will be right out to help. Where's Lord Vermi?"

"He's in the command tent with the Captains, Kaylee Quia."

"Thank you."

She let the flap close and smiled. *That lazy fool won't do his own dirty work.* She did some simple weaves of Water and Air and cleaned herself from the dust that seemed to permeate everywhere in this God-forsaken desert plain. *God, how I have come to hate riding horses.* Leaving her tent, Juventus called her 'sisters' out of their tent.

Gildred, Hamala, and Junis looked as though they tried to clean themselves but still looked haphazard and dusty. *Oh, how the mighty fall.*

"I am going to the command tent. You three will take a little walk East and use Air to cover up any traces of hoofprints, then meet me in the command tent. You will tell me, in front of Vermi, that you cannot locate Bella nor any signs of horse travel."

"How long shall we be?" asked Gildred.

"Oh, let's say…an hour."

"As you wish, sister Kaylee." All three said with unnaturally big grins.

Juventus made her way through the hustle and bustle of soldiers organizing search parties for the prisoner. *A minor distraction, at best. I only hope Rowan uses it wisely.*

Juventus entered a large bleached white cotton tent, housing a large pine folding table that could double for a dining table for eight. Maps were strewn upon the top, and small bags of sand here and there to hold down the many corners. She sauntered up to Vermi in her tight white low-cut riding dress, showing every curve on her body. He had his hands flat on the table, bent over a map showing their current location.

"Trouble?"

Vermi and his two captains looked up from the map at the sultry voice.

"Oh…you. We're busy. If I need your *talents*, I'll call on you."

"Oh, but my Lord Vermi. I had already dispatched my sisters to help."

"You did what?!" Vermi said, almost standing on his toes to meet her eyes.

Juventus put on a gentle smile.

"A guard told me, and I didn't think you would mind the extra help, with their *talents*."

Vermi lowered his head. *That meddlesome woman!* He looked back up at her with ire in his eyes.

"Fine. Just stay out of the way for now," he said, waving a hand at her.

"As you wish, Lord Vermi."

Vermi watched her saunter to one of the folding pine seats along the inside edge of the tent. He cocked his head as he watched her and grasped for the memory that slipped away. Then, finally unable to recall, he let out a sigh and turned back to the captains.

"Have your men circle the camp in both directions. Pay close attention to the ground for hoofprints. Kill on sight."

"As you command, My Lord." In unison, saluting.

Sitting in the chair as regal as a Queen, Juventus watched the exchange, smiling.

Vermi raked his hand through his hair, scratched his goatee, then remembered Kaylee was still in the tent with him. He smoothed his hair back with both hands rather than use Medeis.

"Very well executed, Lord Vermi."

"Don't patronize me, woman. I told you we should have killed her long before."

"True, but then we would not have found out what we did."

"You mean *you* wouldn't have found out. She somehow refused to speak with me."

"Oh, I guess it's just a woman's touch."

Juventus continued to smile at Vermi as he waved another dismissive hand and scoffed.

"Bullshit. You're playing some game."

"Me? A game??" She giggled and leaned forward, exposing more of her breasts.

"Don't feign innocence with me. I have heard you 'Quia' like to pretend to play Ludas Latrun."

"Oh, I assure you, Lord Vermi. I was never any good at that. Besides, you know we Quia are sworn to tell the truth."

"Pah."

Juventus almost laughed out loud at Vermi's growing frustration. *Just like old times.*

She watched him pour over the map, moving small carved pieces from a chessboard this way and that, resetting the pieces, moving them again, and resetting them. She watched as she saw some familiar patterns that Aries had used in the past, unsuccessfully at the time. But this was a new age, and these primitives might not know of them.

The tent's flap opened, and Gildred, Hamala, and Junis entered.

"Have you word, sisters?" Juventus rose from her chair.

"No trace, sister Kaylee." Gildred hung her head.

"Ah, well. You tried."

Vermi slammed a fist down on the table, making some of the chess pieces bounce and fall over.

Juventus turned to him, a placid smile on her face.

"Please let me know if you need any help, Lord Vermi."

"Pah!" Vermi made a dismissive gesture with his hand as he began to right the pieces he had knocked over.

"Come, sisters."

Juventus left the command tent with her ducklings following close behind. *Too easy.*

Chapter 22

Maia awoke before dawn, taking a few moments to stretch and work out the knots in her back from the cot. She poured some water from the pewter pitcher into the matching basin and washed up. She dressed and fixed her hair back into a tight ponytail. She strode out of her tent with purpose.

"It is time."

"Wha?" came a soft voice.

"It is time," Maia repeated outside of Farr and Damara's tent.

"ah…ok…one minute."

Maia lightly tapped her foot on the trampled dry grass, now like straw strewn about the camp.

Damara exited the tent with Farr, both holding their bows and full quivers strapped to their sides.

"Remember, scout only. Do not engage the enemy."

"Yes, Maia Quia." Damara acknowledged. Farr grunted, wiping sleep from his tilted, jewel-like eyes.

"Good. Be careful. Be vigilant."

Maia looked up to the East, and the deep red glow on the horizon gave her a chill. *Red in the morning, sailor take warning.* She marched back to her tent to wake the girls and to go over the plan, yet again.

Farr craned his neck, looking up at Damara.

"Shall we love?"

She smiled down at him and bent over double to kiss him.

They got on their horses and rode southeast in a wide arc, sagebrush almost scraping Damara's shoulders.

Halfway through, Farr pulled up on his reins.

"Whoa."

"What is it, mo chridhe?"

"I have an idea. Hold on…"

Farr rummage through several pockets.

"Ah-ha!"

"What's that?"

"A PHD."

"What?"

"A Personal Handheld Device. Just wait a sec…There. That should work."

"I don't understand."

"There was too much interference because of the magnetic poles and Medeis. So I had to adjust and compensate for the polarity shift and the IFR."

Damara looked at him with a vacant look he recognized when Llyr taught one of his many classes.

"IFR, or Interference Frequency Radiation, can cause fuzzy false images. By fine-tuning the frequency, I tuned it out. Now I can use the PHD to scan ahead in about a fifteen-mile radius."

"Is that an object made from Medeis?"

Farr laughed.

"Ah, no. It's called technology. Similar to how the wheel was developed long ago, or my bow."

"Oh, an inVermion?"

"Sort of. But much more advanced. Let's continue. You lead while I use the PHD."

"As you wish, mo chridhe."

The sun began its harsh beating on the land, and Farr took off his light cloak and rolled it up behind his saddle. The PHD started to vibrate in a pulsing manner.

"Hold up!"

Damara stopped her horse and Farr's horse.

"What is it?"

"There are multiple movements. One large mass on the hill to our right. One small, most likely a single person, moving fast to the east. A small, looks like a pair, circling the large group on the hill, and another large group moving in from the east to the large group on the hill."

"We can assume the large group on the hill is from Meridiem, mo chridhe."

"Yes, I would say so."

"Then who are the others?"

"Not sure. Let's ride more southeast and see who the other large group is."

"Agreed, mo chridhe."

They rode slowly into the hot sunlight as it was halfway to its zenith, Farr shielding his eyes, so he could see the small screen on the PHD.

"hold." He whispered.

Damara stopped the horses again. Farr held out the PHD for her to see four red dots on a topographic grid break off from the large red mass of dots, heading directly for them.

"How far?"

Farr looked at the PHD again.

"Not sure, maybe two miles?"

"If we dismount, we would be more hidden, mo chridhe."

"Me more than you, my love."

Farr smiled up lovingly at her.

"You stay here with the horses. I can move fast and silent in this growth. I'll have the PHD. I can get a quick look and be back before you know it."

Damara shook her head in a futile silent protest.

"Ugh, be careful, mo chridhe."

"Always, my love."

Farr slid off his horse nocked an arrow in the compound bow he designed. Then, stealthily he quickly made his way in the thick sage toward the four red dots on the PHD. It vibrated more and more the closer he got. Farr heard them before he saw them and froze.

Four hunched over black humanoids, thick black bristly hair, and heads like a bat. Pushing each other and snapping razor-sharp teeth like a pack of hyenas. Farr held his breath as they passed within ten feet of him.

They failed to see or smell the tiny Lacerten hiding in the middle of a sage bush. He slowly let out his breath after the Fera passed and made his way back to Damara.

She had dismounted, the sage just covering her head.

"Who were they?"

"Fera. We need to get back to camp. Fast."

Farr took a last look at the PHD and switched it off.

"The way should be clear. Let us ride with alacrity."

They spurred their horses as fast as they could move in the tall, thick brush towards the camp as the sun passed its zenith.

****

"You both know the plan?"

"Yes, Mother." They said in unison.

"Good. Come with me, Aislinn. Good luck Luigh, do what you can, but conserve your strength. Using Medeis can be…taxing."

Aislinn followed Maia, giving a backward glance and small wave to Luigh. Luigh returned the wave, mouthed 'good luck', and was left alone in front of their tent. She let out a big sigh and made her way over to where the infirmary tent was set up. *She better keep Ais safe, or there will be Hell to pay.*

Maia strode so fast that Aislinn had to take a few quick steps now and then to keep up. They reached the front of the camp, just on the edge of a hill. Maia looked over the plain below and let out a breath of resignation. Aislinn looked up, and the hazy red-hot morning sun was just rising to the east. A low rumble caught her attention, and she turned westward and saw the army of Ventus galloping into the thick sage, their long lances held up at a forty-five-degree angle to avoid the brush.

"Will this work, Mother?"

"Just stay by me, child. All will be well."

Maia turned around, faced the camp, and waited as the Parva Frater army saddled up. MacGill rode up to Maia and Aislinn.

"We are ready. You?"

"We will remain here. I will have a good vantage."

"As you wish, Maia Quia."

He turned his horse and raised his right hand. Aislinn could hear Glenn bark out the order to advance, and the Parva Frater army rode down the hill onto the plain.

****

Vermi smiled as he looked through the spyglass on the knoll's edge. *Just like I thought. Simple old tactics. This will be over before lunch.* He let out a laugh.

"Captains! Give the command to advance."

The two captains saluted Vermi and shouted orders as the Meridiem army mounted and rode down into the plain to meet the Parva Frater army.

"May I ask your plan?"

Vermi was startled by the sultry voice behind him. He turned to see Kaylee standing there with her ducklings.

"Ugh. You…again. You have the bad habit of popping up when your least wanted."

He turned back to look over the plain.

"If you want to help, get the boy and bring him to me."

"As you wish, Lord Vermi."

Juventus looked at Hamala, grinning like an idiot at her, and waved her to get Joesiph for Vermi. Hamala curtsied and ran to the camp. She returned moments later, practically dragging Joesiph by his sleeve to the edge of the knoll.

"As you requested, Lord Vermi."

Vermi collapsed the spyglass and tucked it into a pocket, turning to Joesiph.

"Ah, good. Be ready, boy. They are here for you."

Joesiph scowled at the Parva Frater army, a quarter a mile away. Just close enough for him. He took a deep breath and closed his eyes. Vermi saw the glow of Medeis spring up around the boy.

"Good. Now make them pay for your family."

Joesiph's head snapped up, his eyes burning with rage, and he held out his hands towards the plain.

The ground in front of the Parva Frater army erupted in a hail of dirt and rock. The first three lines in the column flew up into the air, horses, and men screaming, MacGill and Glenn among them. The army paused to let the earth settle, most maintaining its formation and moved forward, while a group from the back moved about the scree to help any survivors.

The Meridiem army slowly advanced across the plain as Joesiph took another deep breath.

"Yes, good. Now make them pop."

Vermi almost giggled at the carnage.

Joesiph made a circle motion with his outstretched hands and then made it like he was pulling something apart.

The fourth and fifth row in the Parva Frater army popped in a giant red mist. Armor, horse, and human flesh flying in all directions.

"Now!" Maia shouted at Aislinn.

Aislinn took hold of Medeis and passed control onto Maia.

Juventus saw the bright glow from where she stood. *Did the Conclave arrive already? Impossible!*

Maia furiously wove a web over the remaining rows of Parva Frater men and held out her hands to maintain the weave.

"Hit them again for your Ma!" Vermi squealed with glee, rubbing his hands together, unable to see the female use of Medeis.

Joesiph made another weave to explode the next few rows of Parva Frater. His eyes went wide. Vermi saw the destructive weave bounce off the unseen shield.

"Cursed women!"

He spun on Juventus.

"Can't you do something about that!"

"We could try, but I fear that's a Conclave. Perhaps you could??"

Vermi growled. He held his hand out and pointed over the tops of the Meridiem army. A thin bolt of fire shot out, and the Meridiem army began their charge.

"They will have to drop their shield for their men to fight. When that happens, boy, be ready."

"Yes, Lord Vermi."

****

Luigh paced inside the infirmary tent. She stopped when she felt the ground shake, then she heard the screams. She burst out of the tent at a dead run toward the killing field.

She was almost to where Aislinn and Maia were supposed to be when she was stopped by two soldiers driving a wagon of wounded men.

"Mistress Quia! Help us!"

Luigh saw the bright glow around Aislinn and Maia, then turned to the wagon.

"Don't move!"

"As you wish, Mistress Quia."

Luigh examined the groaning men, embraced Medeis, and began healing them. She made her way from man to man, easing their pain, mending broken bones, and sealing up tears in their skin. Her last patient was unconscious. She recognized the older man by the scar on the left side of his face. She checked for a pulse and found it weak but there, his breathing shallow and raspy. *Broken ribs, possibly punctured lung, and internal bleeding.* She placed her hands over him and concentrated. Sweat began to bead on her forehead. Finally, Glenn's breathing eased, and his body shivered. Luigh let out a sigh, then she was knocked out of the wagon by the concussion wave.

****

Juventus Joined with Gildred, Hamala, and Junis. She looked to the sky above where the bright glow was on the other hill. She made a swirling motion with her hands, then swiftly pulled them down.

****

Aislinn was knocked back a good twenty feet from where she was standing. Her eyes fluttered as she saw the blue of the sky fade to black.

Luigh got to her knees and quickly looked to where Aislinn and Maia had been standing. A good ten-foot radius of the area was sunken in as if compressed. Luigh looked to the left of the depression and saw Aislinn lying on the ground, not moving.

****

Juventus saw the bright glow wink out on the other hilltop.

"You're welcome."

"You broke a Conclave?"

"I…distracted them."

"Finally, a use for you. Boy, be ready to erupt the ground behind the enemy to stop them from escaping."

****

Luigh scrambled on all fours to the unmoving body of Aislinn. The sound of metal clashing on metal in the field below faded as her own heartbeat grew louder in her ears. She put her fingers to the side of Aislinn's neck. A pulse. Luigh moved her hand to under Aislinn's nose. Breath. Luigh sat back on her heels and caught her own breath. *That WOMAN!* The anger started to well up from deep inside her, rising with her as she stood. Luigh walked back to where the depression was and looked for Maia. There was no sign of her, but something did catch her eye.

A bright glow on the other hilltop. Luigh reached out with all her anger at the sky with thick strands of Fire, Air, Earth, and Water intertwining to form a large tight cable, and pulled down.

Farr and Damara galloped up to the camp from the eastern side of the hill, their horses lathered. Something purple lying on the hillside caught Farr's eye, and he made for it. He sprang off his horse before it could even come to a stop and ran to the purple figure of Maia.

"bl..ow…the…horn."

"Horn? What horn?"

Farr's tilted almond jewel eyes widened. *The HORN! How could I forget it!* Farr ran back to his horse and rifled through his saddlebag, pulling out the silver bugle that seemed to twinkle with starlight. He put his mouth to the mouthpiece that fit his diminutive lips perfectly and blew.

****

Juventus and Vermi knew it. They had heard that note long ago, and it still made them shudder in fear as if they were facing an Arbitrium. Neither noticed the grey swirling clouds above.

The Meridiem army floundered at the sound of the horn, horses throwing their riders. The Parva Frater men fought with renewed vigor and strength.

Lightning came crashing down on the hilltop, killing Hamala in a bright blue flash, set many tents on fire, and dirt fling high into the air to come raining down. Vermi turned and began to run back to the camp.

Juventus shaking from the bleat of the horn, reached out with Medeis and shielded Gildred, and snapped Junis' neck in one smooth motion. Then, she tied the shield off on Gildred and ran after Vermi. *Oh no. Not so fast, you vermin.*

Joesiph turned around in circles, unsure which way to run, as Gildred fell to her knees and wailed at the loss of Medeis.

****

As Damara picked up a limp Maia, Farr put the horn back into his saddlebag.

"She needs help, mo chridhe."

"Up the hill, to Luigh, fast love!"

The two scrambled up the hill to find Luigh staring out over the bloody field, a motionless Aislinn a few feet behind her on the ground. Damara gently laid Maia next to Aislinn. Farr ran up to Luigh.

"Luigh!"

Luigh's jaw set, stared at the opposite hilltop, her heartbeat still thundering in her head.

"LUIGH!"

Luigh blinked hard and shook her head, looking from left to right, her Medeis winking out.

Farr tugged on her sleeve, and she looked down at him, surprised.

"Luigh! Maia's hurt. She needs you. NOW!"

Farr tugged on her sleeve again, getting her to slowly move towards the two women lying on the ground. Luigh's legs felt like they were glued to the ground, and she had to almost pull them with her hands to bend and move.

Luigh blinked and rubbed her eyes as if she was just waking up from a dream. *No. More like a nightmare.* She knelt down beside Maia. *I can do nothing. We don't owe her anything. We can be free.* She looked at Aislinn, her breathing was regular, but she was still unconscious. *Ugh, I'd never hear the end of it.* Luigh surrendered to Medeis, took hold of it, put her hands over Maia, and felt out with microscopic tendrils of Air and Water. Luigh added tendrils of Fire where necessary to cauterize some internal bleeding and fuse a few ribs. Maia's breathing became more regular. Luigh wiped the sweat from her brow.

"She'll be fine. Help me bring them back to our tent. They need rest, and I need to help the others."

Farr nodded, and he got one of the guards on medic detail to help carry Aislinn as Damara picked up Maia.

Farr watched as Luigh walked away toward the infirmary tent. *She totally paused at helping Maia! That is new and very much not like her.*

Chapter 23

A islinn groaned almost as loudly as her stomach as she turned in her cot.

"What happened?"

"You and I were apparently thrown several yards. Here, you need to eat," came a familiar voice.

Aislinn opened her eyes to see Maia holding a tray. Aislinn pushed herself up to a seated position.

"How'd I get here??"

"We were carried. That is, after Luigh healed us. Now eat. You will need to regain your strength."

"Ugh, is this how Rowan feels all the time?? How does he not pass out from hunger?"

Maia chuckled.

"It is a wonder. Now eat, child."

Aislinn tore into the meal of dried venison, cheese, and bread like a ravenous animal. With crumbs on Aislinn's face and down the front of her dress, Farr, Damara, and Luigh came into the tent.

"And how's my patient?"

"umph," Aislinn swallowed a huge bite, "better, thanks to you, I hear."

"Good, and you Maia?"

Maia cocked an eyebrow at the first name basis.

"I am better. Thank you, child."

"Good. Now, what's next?"

"Well, next is we see an old friend."

"You have friends?"

"Sarcasm aside, I do, and you would be well advised to hold your tongue. She is not as…accommodating as I."

Luigh looked at Aislinn and raised her eyebrows mockingly. Aislinn shrugged as she tore into another slice of cheese.

Luigh turned back to Maia.

"When do we leave?"

"As soon as Aislinn is on her feet, child."

"What about the group from Occursum? Shouldn't we wait for them?"

"No, child. They can deal with the man who can use Medeis. He won't get far now that he is alone."

Luigh narrowed her eyes at Maia.

"What are you hiding?"

Maia sighed.

"It would be better if we meet up with my friend and get a decent meal and rest."

Luigh put a finger to her lip and thought for a moment.

"One day, Maia Quia, your game will bite you in your ass."

"Perhaps, child. But today is not that day."

Aislinn started to laugh and almost choked on a piece of bread. She sputtered and coughed as Luigh and Maia looked to make sure they didn't need to hit her back or something. Farr brought her some water from the side table.

"Thank you, Farr. I think I'm ready to go, Mother."

"As you wish, child."

Maia turned to the others.

"Get packed. We leave in five minutes."

Farr and Damara gave a small wave as they left the tent to pack. The sun had set a few hours earlier, and the evening air was beginning to cool. Farr reached out and took Damara's hand as they went into their tent without saying a word.

They regrouped outside of Maia's tent, everyone packed. Farr looked up at Maia.

"What about the Fera?"

"We should be able to avoid what's left of them. The remnants of the Ventus army that ran into a group to the West, causing them to miss the onslaught, added to what's left of the Parva Frater army should rout them. Now that we know there were two groups of Fera, thanks to you." *The bigger question is how they were able to get so far South without being noticed.*

Farr blushed.

"Now, let us get to our horses."

Under a cloudless night sky, they were able to ride northeast for most of the night under a full moon. Maia suddenly slowed the group after several hours.

"We are coming up on her house soon. Remember, let me do all the talking. If asked, be respectful."

Farr saw the farmhouse before the others and pointed out the direction. It was a small house, with a barn and a small vegetable patch. Maia led the group to the barn.

"Farr, will you and Damara take care of the horses?"

Farr nodded. They all dismounted and gave the reins to Farr and Damara to lead the horses into the barn. Maia led Aislinn and Luigh to the front door of the house.

Maia knocked three times on the front door and waited.

"Who is it?" came a curmudgeonly voice.

"Maia Quia."

"Fine. Come in."

Maia opened the door and entered with Aislinn and Luigh in tow. The house wasn't much bigger on the inside. The living room and kitchen were combined with a stone fireplace roaring with a newly started fire. A few single tapered candles were lit around the living room-kitchen area. There weren't many places to sit; two high-backed cushioned chairs and a loveseat surrounded a small pine coffee table. There was a small four-paned window in two walls, and the rest was taken up by floor-to-ceiling bookcases stuffed with books of varying size and age. There was a closed pine door to a backroom that Aislinn assumed was a bedroom.

"Well, as I live and still breath! Why on Earth are you here?"

"This..."

Maia stepped aside with her arm out, presenting Aislinn and Luigh.

The old woman's eyes widened. She groaned as she got up from her chair.

"Ooohhh. Let me see what you have brought."

The old woman shuffled closer to Aislinn and Luigh, invading their personal space as she looked them up and down. They both wanted to rub their noses from the musty smell from the old woman, the books, or both.

"They are strong. Yes, very strong. Are they trained?"

"Not fully. That is why we are here."

"Yes. Yes. Without Angus, I see."

"Yes. I would ask you to take these two to the Spire whilst I go meet up with Angus."

"Oh? You would have me go back there?? That's a big ask, child."

The old lady put her hands on her hips and squared off with Maia.

"I wouldn't ask, if the need wasn't important, Mother."

The old woman's eyes widened.

"you found him!"

"I did."

"Yes. YES! Come in and warm up. I'll cook up some eggs and bacon. You must be starved! I'm Kathrein Quia girls, and I taught this one all she knows."

Kathrein thumbed a gnarled finger at Maia and cackled as she shuffled over to the kitchen area.

The door opened, and Farr and Damara entered.

Kathrein looked past Luigh to see the two newcomers.

"Why, Maia, you do like to still surprise me."

"Allow me to make introductions. Mother, Luigh, and Aislinn, you met; these two are Farr and Damara."

"Yes. A Caitheness and a…"

"A *friend*."

"Hmm. 'Friend', huh. Alright, Maia. I'll allow you that secret…for now. Hah! Two powerful humans, a Caitheness and a 'friend'. The Phoenix sure arrives in style."

Kathrein turned back to the kitchen and resumed making an early breakfast.

Here ends
The Clarion Call

Epilogue

Vermi ran between the bleached white empty tents. Crashing lightning behind him. He grabbed hold of Medeis and made the weave several yards in front of him. The air began to shimmer as the portal formed until it was mirror smooth and looked into a darkened room. He stepped through at a dead run and laughed. *I made it!*

He watched the portal start to close, then felt the shock as someone else had taken hold of the weave as the portal regained its form. Kaylee stepped through.

"You?? But how?!?"

"Oh, you silly little man. You still have no clue??"

Juventus let all her weaves around her go as she retook her given image.

"NO! YOU CAN'T BE HERE!"

"Oh yes, my little rat."

Juventus let the portal close behind her as the lightning stopped booming on the ill-fated hilltop. She did a quick weave, and Vermi's eyes went even wider as he fell to his knees whimpering.

"Noooo. Pllleeeeaaassse. I'll do whatever you want."

Juventus smiled and almost purred as she tussled his hair.

"Of course, you will, my pet rat. Of course."

She grabbed a handful of his hair as she looked around the dimly lit room. She could feel the oppressive humidity and taste the salt air as she looked around the room made of round stones and mortar.

"Where have you led me, my pet rat?"

"To, to, home."

"Home?"

"What they now call Ab Oriente."

Juventus let go of his hair and let out a hearty laugh.

"Oh, you ugly beautiful rat. How fortunate this is for you!"

Vermi swallowed hard. In no way was this fortunate for him.

****

Bella tried to whimper, but the gag in her mouth was solidly tight. She looked around the tiny bedroom. Her hands and feet were also bound tight with rope. She delivered her message but couldn't do the last directive of her mistress; commit suicide. Oh, how she wanted to. Unable to use Medeis, she was helpless and empty. Even though she could have easily overpowered the old woman, the Coacta prevented it. Instead, she lay on a musty pine floor in a tiny dark bedroom as the smells of cooking bacon and eggs permeated the air.

Glossary

Adversus -

(Ad-ver-sus) 12 Medeis users from before the Breaking that made a connection to The Blackness and created Viventem. Thought to be sealed in the void between Runcina Terrae and The Blackness' plane.

Aeneas -

(A-ne-as) The second weakest male Adversus. Killed by Luigh after he defeated Rowan in a duel.

AF Power

Akashic Field Power, see Medeis

Aislinn Inion -

(Ash-lin In-yon) Communications specialist of the Novus and cousin to Coinneach. Called Ais (Ash) for short.

Angus Gleidhidh -

(Glee-ah-did) Companion of Maia Quia. From Magna Frater.

Arbitrium -

(Ar-bi-tri-um) An unemotional, except when killing, highly intelligent Viventem. Created by Adversus using Medeis. Dark, light-absorbing skin allows it to be almost undetectable in low and no light. It was used as a command creature for

lesser Viventem. Has
the ability to sense
Medeis in close
proximity, induce
directed fear, and can
only be killed by
beheading. Usually used
to command 10 Beluinus
and would rather ride
than walk.

Aries -

Strongest Adversus
sealed in the Void. One
of the original six.

Baile Atha Cliath -

(Baily A-tha Cl-ee-th)
Capitol of Septentriones.

Beluinus -

(Be-lune-is) A brutish
rock-colored, heavily
muscled humanoid with
very thick skin that acts
as medium armor, able
to resist most projectiles
and cuts, and little hair.
Created by Adversus

using Medeis. It wears light armor for looks rather than protection, has average intelligence, has the strength of 10 humans, and takes orders from Arbitrium. Usually used to command groups of 10 Fera.

Blaine Caisteal -

(Kay-steal) Prince of Parva Frater.

Blue Septem -

Female Medeis users, devoted to scientific applications of Medeis. Some have Gleidhidh.

Brianna Caisteal -

(Kay-steal) Queen of Parva Frater.

Brighid Quia -	(Brig-id Kia) Purple Septem and advisor to Parva Frater.
Brown Septem -	Female Medeis users, devoted to Archeology and Bibliography. Few have Gleidhidh.
Caden Thorburn -	Captain of the Guard in Parva Frater.
Caedmon Caisteal -	(Kad-muhn Kay-steal) King of Parva Frater.
Caitheness -	Large, primarily hairy, humanoids that live in Woodlands and rarely venture out of them. They have an uncanny connection to nature.

Caitlin Thornton -   Princess of Septentriones.

Caryn Thornton -   Queen of Septentriones.

Cecilia Quia -   (Kia) Advisor to Septentriones. Red Septem.

Coinneach -   (Con-ak) Mechanic of the Novus, cousin of Aislinn, and best friend to Rowan.

Coacta -   A form of mind compulsion weaving using Medeis. Extremely difficult to master and risks the target to be lobotomized or brain dead.

Cullum Gleidhidh -   (Cul-lum Glee-ah-did) Guardian of Brighid Quia.

Cutis Praesidium -   A complicated weave of Medeis that protects the user's skin from most elements. The more intricate the weave, the better the protection. Most common protection is from UV rays and extreme temperature.

Damara -   Caitheness female. Daughter of Elder Gildred.

Deas Daingneach -   (De-as Dain-ak) Capitol of Parva Frater.

Douglas MacGill -   Lieutenant of the Guard in Parva Frater.

Dissimulare -

A complicated weaving
of disguise using Medeis.

Dele Vitam -

A devastating weaving of
Medeis from the War of
Power. So devastating
that only two modern
Purple Quia know how.
A brilliant bluish-white
beam of energy that
erases all it touches from
existence, leaving only a
nuclear shadow. The
stronger the Medeis user,
the more devastating it
can be.

Elder Gildred -

Caitheness male. Oldest
and leader of Damara's
Woodland, and her
father.

Fearghal -

(Farr-el) Lacerten male.
Mechanic and co-

designer of the Novus. Called Farr for short. Indigenous to Proxima b.

Fera -

(Fe-ra) Wild, cannibalistic, unintelligent Viventem. Created by Adversus using Medeis. Small humanoids as strong as two humans, covered in thick black hair like light armor, bat-like ears, eyes, noses, razor-sharp teeth with toxic saliva, and razor-sharp claws. They looked hunched over as if the top half of their bodies were large and attached to much smaller bottoms. Normally controlled by Beluinus but can roam in small groups.

Gleidhidh -   (Glee-ah-did) Guardians of Quia. Connected to Quia by Vinculum. Have enhanced stamina, strength, and able to sense Viventem. Not all Quia have Gleidhidh; some have more than one, most have only one.

Green Septem -   Female Medeis users, devoted to Agriculture. Most have Gleidhidh.

Introitus Ad Infernum -   (In-troit-us Ad Infernum) Mountain in the furthest northeast corner of the continent. Where the Runcina Terrae and The Blackness are the closest.

Iter -   A weaving of Medeis that creates a portal by folding space-time distance and allows the user to travel instantaneously from one location to another on a single plane of existence. The user must be able to form an exact image of both locations to successfully form the portal.

Juventus -   Second strongest Adversus, and strongest female Adversus. One of the original six.

Liam Thornton -   Prince of Septentriones.

Luighseach Nighean -   (Lee-sak Nee-han) Commander of the Novus. Called Luigh (Lee) for short.

Ludus Latrun -   The Great Game of schemes. From the War

of Power but used in
Occursum and Ad
Oriente.

Llyr -

(Lear) Lacerten male.
Designer of the Novus
and mentor to Farr.
Indigenous to Proxima
b.

Maia Quia -

(My-ya Ki-a) Medeis user
of the Purple Septem
from Ab Oriente.

Medeis -

(Me-de-is) The power
wielded by Quia and
Adversus. A link to the
Akashic Field. Gives
extended life and
abilities. Four main
elements: Earth, Fire,
Water, Wind/Spirit. All
Medeis users can use all
elements, but Earth and
Fire come more naturally
to male users, while

	Water and Wind/Spirit come more naturally to female users.
Naill Glenn -	(Nye-all) Master of Arms of Parva Frater.
Novus -	Scout ship that crews six members. Has an experimental Super Luminous Drive.
Obelisk -	A large 20-foot-tall pillar with runes carved into it. A Medeis user can travel to different dimensions and locations in the same dimension based on the runes.
Obiectum -	(O-bee-ec-tium) Objects made with Medeis. Three levels, Summas (high), Medi (Middle),

Infirma (weak). Some can be used without activation with Medeis.

Occulta Potentia -	A weaving of Medeis to hide the user's true ability or full potential. Depending on how intricate the weave, the more hidden the Medeis power.

Primus Princeps -	The highest-ranking elected official in Occursum and the leader of Quia in the Spire. It is normally a lifetime term until retirement.

Portuaqnem -	(Por-tu-aq-nem) Large gap between the North and East Mountains.

Purple Septem -   Battle Quia that hunt
                       Viventem. They all have
                       Gleidhidh.

Quia -   (Ki-a) Medeis users that
                       oppose Adversus and
                       The Darkness.

Red Septem -   Male Medeis hunters.
                       None have Gleidhidh.

Rowan Sohnaues -   (Rowan Son-(h)ouse)
                       Pilot of the Novus.

Runcina Terrae -   (Run-cina Terr-rae)
                       Earth Plane of existence.

Scriba Ad Primum -   The Secretary and
                       Holder of Keys to the
                       Spire. Second in
                       Command to Primus
                       Princeps. An appointed
                       position by the Primus

Princeps. Normally a lifetime position until retirement.

Septem -   (Sep-tem) Area of study or affinity for female Quia. There are seven Septem: White, Purple, Green, Yellow, Blue, Red, and Brown.

Servire Et Tueri -   Oath taken by all Quia using a Summas Obiectum. Three parts: Do no harm to Quia, Civilians, and Caitheness unless in defense of life. Make no weapons of war. Tell no lie.

Shades -   Humans that have sold their souls to The Blackness for power.

The Blackness -   A being from another plane. Discovered by Adversus. Wants to control Runcina Terrae.

Thomas McDermid -   Captain of the Queen's Guard in Septentriones.

Tiernan Sullivan -   Innkeeper and owner of the Unicorn in Baile Atha Cliath. Called Sully for short.

Vastante -   (Va-ston-tay) Area north of the Northern Mountains. Corrupted by The Blackness and controlled by Viventem.

Vermi -   Weakest male Adversus. Not part of the original six. Idolized Aires.

Vinculum -   (Vin-cul-um) Connection
                     between Quia and
                     Gleidhidh. Emotions
                     can pass through the
                     connection, as well as a
                     sense of location and
                     well-being.

Viventem -   (Vi-ven-tem) Creatures
                     created by Adversus by
                     the knowledge given
                     from The Blackness.

Void -   Space between planes
                     where Adversus were
                     trapped at the end of the
                     War of Power.

White Septem -   Female Medeis users,
                     devoted to Diplomacy
                     and Negotiation. Rarely
                     have Gleidhidh.

Woodland -	Area that consists of great redwood-like broadleaf conifers where Caitheness live.
Woodland Portal -	An archway in the center of a Woodland village created by Medeis. Connects Woodlands to each other. Known as 'The Path'.
Yellow Septem -	Medical Quia. Healers. Some have Gleidhidh.

About The Author

R obert Krause was born in New Rochelle, NY, in 1971, but was raised in Carmel, NY, where he graduated high school. Upon graduating from Western New England University in Springfield, MA, with a Bachelor of Science in Biology, he went on to Graduate coursework in Developmental Biology at Central Connecticut State University in New Britain, CT. He had many different employment paths, from Laboratory Technician at Abbott Laboratories in North Chicago to Director of Operations at an optical imaging company in NYC. He worked on, at the time, Top Secret documentation from World War II reparations

from Swiss Bank in NYC and was a High School
Biology teacher in Pawling, NY, winning Who's
Who of American High School Teachers twice in
his 4 years. His last and probably most prolonged
employment was as a Deputy Sheriff in rural
Central and Northeastern Montana; he says it
fulfilled all his ADD dreams, as it was never the
same nor routine. Robert is married to his wife
Caryn and has two children, Caitlin and William,
from a previous marriage. He enjoys getting
together with friends from High School to role-
play and plays the bagpipes in several local bands.
He competed in bagpipes and won many band
competitions with the Putnam County Sheriff's
pipe band in his younger years, earning a grade 3
status in band competition. Robert played
bagpipes for President George W. Bush on the
U.S. Capitol steps, led the Royal Canadian
Mounted Police, played on the U.S. Coast Guard
Cutter 'Eagle'. He still plays with local pipe bands
for fun and teaches solo players and the FDNY
EMS pipe band.

Piper Publishing, LLC

www.piperpublishing.org

Instagram

@robertkrause_author

Facebook

RuncinaTerraeBooks

www.ingramcontent.com/pod-product-compliance
Lightning Source LLC
Chambersburg PA
CBHW051159190726
48288CB00006B/1724